Love Forgotten
Lost Love Investigation

Part 1: The Lost Love

Prologue: The Ephesus Parallel   2
Chapter 1: A Church Without Love   5
Chapter 2: The World Falls Apart   8
Chapter 3: The Visitors   11
Chapter 4: The Prophetic Warning   15
Chapter 5: The Lost Virtue   19
Chapter 6: The Investigators   23

Part 2: The Search for Love

Chapter 7: The First Clue   27
Chapter 8: Revisiting the Past   32
Chapter 9: The Hardened Hearts   36
Chapter 10: A Journey Through Denominations   41
Chapter 11: The Mirror of the World   45
Chapter 12: The Prayer Revival   49
Chapter 13: The Missing Ingredient   53
Chapter 14: The Battle Within   57

Part 3: The Spiritual War

Chapter 15: The Enemy's Agenda   62
Chapter 16: The Power of Unity   66
Chapter 17: A Vision of the Bride   70
Chapter 18: The World Speaks   74
Chapter 19: The Cost of Love   73
Chapter 20: The Underground Church   84
Chapter 21: The Spiritual Weapons   88

Part 4: Restoring Love

Chapter 22: The First Church Transformed   93
Chapter 23: The Ripple Effect   98
Chapter 24: The Ultimate Test   102
Chapter 25: Love in Action   107
Chapter 26: The Final Push   112
Chapter 27: The Bride Awakens   117
Chapter 28: The World is Watching   122
Epilogue: Love Restored   127

Part 1: The Lost Love

Prologue: The Ephesus Parallel

It began with a single letter.

The envelope was unmarked, bearing no postage stamp, no return address. It simply appeared—on pulpits, church desks, and even mailboxes of the faithful—simultaneously across the globe. The handwriting was delicate, almost ancient, with ink that seemed to shimmer faintly in the light. The letter read:

> "To the church:
> I hold this against you: You have forsaken the love you had at first.
> Remember the height from which you have fallen!
> Repent and do the things you did at first.
> If you do not repent, I will come to you and remove your lampstand from its place.
> Revelation 2:4-5."

No signature. No explanation. Just a solemn warning.

At first, many dismissed it as a hoax, a modern-day attempt to stir up fear. But within days, the words of the letter began to manifest in startling, inexplicable ways. Churches reported an eerie stillness during their services—no sense of joy, no spirit of connection. Congregants began to murmur that the love in their hearts felt distant, like a fire dwindling to embers. Long-held grudges resurfaced, and divisions deepened between believers.

Meanwhile, outside the church walls, the world's chaos grew. Nations faltered under the weight of corruption, injustice, and despair. The news was saturated with stories of unprovoked violence, families torn apart, and governments collapsing into disorder. It was as though the earth itself sensed the absence of something vital—a force that held the darkness at bay.

In one church in the heart of a bustling city, Pastor Jonathan held the letter in trembling hands. His wife, Sarah, watched from the front pew, her face pale with concern. The congregation before him sat in restless silence, their eyes hollow, their souls seemingly drained of light. Jonathan tried to preach as he always did, but the words tasted bitter in his mouth. The scripture he'd studied for years felt lifeless in his grasp.

Across the street, a young woman stumbled into the church. Her clothes were torn, and her eyes bore the weight of desperation. She had been running from something—or someone—and instinctively sought refuge within these sacred walls. But as she stood in the doorway, she hesitated. The love and safety she expected to find within the church felt absent, replaced by an oppressive, unspoken judgment emanating from those inside.

"What's happening to us?" Sarah whispered to Jonathan after the service. He had no answer.

The mysterious letter was only the beginning. As more reports poured in of supernatural disturbances—churches experiencing unexplainable power outages during worship, prayer meetings interrupted by strange phenomena—it became clear: this was no hoax. The words of Revelation 2:4-5 were not just a warning—they were a call to action.

Something precious had been lost, and unless it was found again, the church risked losing everything.

The question remained: *Where is love?*

And so, a journey began—a quest to uncover the truth about the missing love and to restore the flame that had once burned so brightly in the hearts of God's people. But as the church struggled to find its way back, the world's chaos only deepened, and time was running out.

Would the church awaken in time to fulfill its mission? Or would the lampstands be removed, one by one, leaving the world in darkness forever?

Chapter 1: A Church Without Love

Pastor Jonathan adjusted the microphone on the podium, his heart heavy as he gazed out over the congregation. Rows of familiar faces stared back at him, but their expressions were indifferent, detached. Some fidgeted with their phones; others whispered to each other, barely paying attention. The sanctuary, once alive with vibrant worship and heartfelt fellowship, felt more like a museum—cold, sterile, and quiet.

The worship team had just stepped down after an uninspired set of songs, their voices devoid of passion. Not long ago, those songs would have brought tears and hands lifted high in surrender. Now, the congregation sang out of habit, if at all. Jonathan's sermons, once met with hearty "Amens" and enthusiastic engagement, were now greeted with polite nods or blank stares.

He flipped open his Bible, the same well-worn one he'd used since seminary, and tried to muster his usual energy. But as the words of Scripture flowed from his mouth, they felt flat. It wasn't that he lacked preparation—Jonathan always prepared diligently—but lately, the messages seemed to lack power, as though the Spirit had withdrawn His hand.

Midway through his sermon, he glanced at his wife, Sarah, sitting in her usual spot near the front. Her eyes were closed, her lips moving silently in prayer. She had always been his greatest supporter, his spiritual anchor. But even Sarah had grown restless over the past few months. He could sense it in her quiet sighs, the way she lingered in the kitchen after dinner, deep in thought.

After the service ended, the congregation filtered out quickly, exchanging brief pleasantries before heading to their cars.

There was no lingering, no laughter echoing in the halls, no signs of the close-knit family they had once been.

Jonathan joined Sarah in the empty sanctuary as she gathered her things.

"Another sermon, another exodus," he said, attempting a weak smile.

Sarah looked at him, her face serious. "Jonathan, we need to talk."

He nodded, sensing where this was going. They had been having variations of this conversation for weeks.

"We're missing something," Sarah said, her voice low but firm. "And it's not just here—it's everywhere. The churches, the people... it's like we've forgotten what it means to love. To really love."

Jonathan sat down beside her, rubbing his temples. "I don't know what to do, Sarah. I preach the Word, I organize events, I visit the sick. What more can I do?"

Sarah placed a hand on his arm. "It's not about programs or activities. When I was on the streets, sharing the gospel, I didn't have a building, a budget, or a schedule. I just had love—raw, relentless love for the broken and the lost. And people responded to that. They knew it was real. But here..." She gestured to the empty sanctuary. "Here, it's all rules and rituals. There's no fire, no passion. It's like we've replaced the heart of the gospel with a checklist."

Jonathan leaned back in the pew, staring up at the ceiling. He wanted to argue, to defend the church he had spent his life building, but deep down, he knew she was right. He had felt it too—that gradual drift from passion to performance, from love to obligation.

"What do we do?" he asked, his voice barely above a whisper.

Sarah smiled faintly. "We start by praying. Not the usual prayers we've been saying, but real, gut-wrenching prayers. We need to ask God to show us what's missing and what needs to change. And we need to be ready for whatever He reveals."

Jonathan nodded slowly, the weight of her words settling on him. For the first time in years, he felt a spark of hope—fragile, but real.

As they locked up the church and stepped into the cool evening air, Jonathan couldn't shake the feeling that something big was coming. He didn't know what it was or how it would change their lives, but he knew one thing for sure: the church couldn't go on like this.

Something had to give. And it had to start with them.

Chapter 2: The World Falls Apart

The morning news blared from the old television in Pastor Jonathan's office. The images were chaotic: floods devastating coastal cities, riots erupting in urban centers, governments on the brink of collapse. Headlines scrolled across the screen like a relentless drumbeat of despair:

- **"Record-Breaking Floods Leave Millions Homeless"**
- **"Economic Meltdown: Nations Declare Emergency"**
- **"Violence Escalates as Communities Collapse"**

Jonathan rubbed his temples, the weight of the world's turmoil pressing down on him. It wasn't just the global disasters that unsettled him—it was the people. Fear and hopelessness were etched into their faces as they crowded the streets, desperate for answers, clinging to false promises from corrupt leaders and self-proclaimed saviors.

His phone buzzed on the desk, interrupting his thoughts. A text message from Sarah read: *Attendance was even lower today at Bible study. People are losing hope, Jonathan.*

He glanced at his calendar. Two months ago, their Sunday services had been full. Now, rows of pews sat empty. The midweek Bible studies, once lively and engaging, were down to a handful of attendees. Even the faithful seemed to be slipping away, seeking solace elsewhere.

That evening, Sarah returned home from her errands, a troubled look on her face.

"I stopped by the food pantry," she began, setting down a bag of groceries. "There was a line wrapped around the block. People are desperate, Jonathan. And not just for food—they're desperate for peace. But they're not coming to the church anymore."

Jonathan sighed. "I know. They're turning to the world instead—self-help gurus, political movements, social media influencers. Everyone's selling a solution, and none of it lasts."

Sarah sat across from him at the dining table, her eyes searching his. "Do you think they see the church as irrelevant now? Like we don't have what they need?"

Jonathan hesitated. It was a question he had been asking himself for weeks. The truth was painful: the church, once a refuge for the hurting and lost, had become a place of rituals and routines, disconnected from the real struggles of the people it was meant to serve.

The next day, Jonathan visited the hospital to pray with an elderly member of his congregation. As he walked through the corridors, he overheard snippets of conversations—patients and families talking about their fears, their frustrations, their doubts.

"Where's God in all of this?" a young man muttered as he paced outside a waiting room. "If He's real, why does the world feel so broken?"

Jonathan paused, his heart sinking. He didn't have an easy answer. The chaos in the world felt overwhelming, even to him.

After leaving the hospital, he drove past a large billboard advertising a new self-help seminar: **"Discover Inner Peace: Unlock Your True Potential!"** The bright, glossy ad promised everything people longed for—hope, healing, fulfillment—but it was just another worldly illusion.

He thought of his own congregation. Even some of his most faithful members had stopped attending. He heard whispers of them joining yoga retreats, meditation groups, or even political rallies in search of something to cling to. The gospel of Jesus Christ, it seemed, was no longer enough.

That evening, Jonathan and Sarah sat together in the living room, their Bibles open between them.

"The world is falling apart, and we're losing the people who need us most," Sarah said, her voice trembling. "How did we get here, Jonathan? How did the church lose its place as the answer to all of this?"

Jonathan shook his head, his voice heavy with sorrow. "We forgot how to love. And without love, what do we have to offer? Rules? Tradition? None of that can compete with the noise out there."

Sarah leaned back, staring at the ceiling. "I think it's worse than we realize. The world is spiraling because the church isn't doing its job. We're supposed to be the light, the salt. But we've gone dim."

Jonathan sat in silence, her words echoing in his mind. If the church had lost its love, its passion, and its power, what hope was there for the world?

As the clock ticked into the night, a quiet but unshakable conviction grew in Jonathan's heart. They couldn't sit by and let things continue this way. The church needed revival—not just in numbers, but in purpose, in spirit, in love.

But where would they even begin? The world was broken, and the church seemed powerless to fix it.

Chapter 3: The Visitors

Sunday morning began like any other. Pastor Jonathan stood in the foyer, greeting the trickle of congregants with a polite smile as they filed into the sanctuary. The worship team was warming up, and the faint strains of a keyboard echoed through the building. Everything was as routine as it could be.

Then, they arrived.

The group came in a noisy cluster—six of them, dressed in mismatched, ragged clothing. Tattoos, piercings, and colorful hair made them stand out instantly. A tall man with a leather jacket and a cigarette tucked behind his ear held the door open for the others. A young woman with bright pink hair clutched a tattered backpack, her eyes darting nervously around the room. Beside her, a middle-aged man wearing a threadbare hoodie walked with a slight limp, his face weathered by years of hardship.

They didn't fit the typical mold of the church's usual visitors. Jonathan saw the heads of his congregation turn in unison, their murmurs barely concealed. He felt the tension rise as the group hesitated just inside the entrance, clearly unsure if they were welcome.

Jonathan stepped forward quickly, extending a hand. "Welcome! I'm Pastor Jonathan. We're glad you're here."

The man in the leather jacket shook his hand firmly, though his gaze remained cautious. "Thanks, Pastor. We're, uh... just looking for a place to sit."

Jonathan nodded warmly. "You're in the right place. Come on in."

As the group moved toward the back pews, Jonathan noticed the looks from his congregation—furtive glances, raised eyebrows, a few whispered exchanges. He felt a pang of disappointment but chose to focus on the newcomers.

During the service, the visitors sat quietly, occasionally whispering among themselves. The congregation, on the other hand, was restless. Jonathan could feel the unspoken discomfort radiating from the pews as he preached.

After the benediction, most of the church members filed out quickly, avoiding eye contact with the group. Jonathan watched as Mrs. Elkins, a longtime member, walked past the newcomers with a tight-lipped smile before whispering to another member, "What kind of people do they think we are letting anyone just walk in here?"

Jonathan gritted his teeth but didn't respond. He turned to see Sarah approaching the visitors, her face alight with warmth. She extended her hand to the man in the leather jacket.

"Hi, I'm Sarah. It's so nice to meet you all."

The man hesitated before taking her hand. "I'm Mike. These are my friends. We just… we needed a place to go. Things have been rough."

Sarah's smile didn't waver. "You're welcome here. If there's anything you need—prayer, food, someone to talk to—please let us know."

The young woman with pink hair spoke up, her voice barely above a whisper. "Thanks. It's been hard to find places where… where people don't look at us like we're trash."

Sarah's eyes softened. "You're not trash. You're loved, more than you know."

As the visitors lingered in the back, Jonathan overheard snippets of conversation from the congregation.

"They don't belong here," one man muttered. "What if they're here to cause trouble?"

"They smell like alcohol," another whispered. "Is this really the kind of crowd we want?"

Jonathan felt anger rising in his chest. Had the church really come to this? Was this the love they claimed to represent?

He walked over to the group, joining Sarah. "We're so glad you came today. Really. Please come back anytime."

Mike nodded, his guarded expression softening. "Thanks, Pastor. We'll see."

As they left, Jonathan watched them disappear down the street, their presence a stark contrast to the neatly dressed members of his congregation.

That afternoon, Jonathan and Sarah sat together at the kitchen table. The tension from the morning still lingered.

"They didn't feel welcome," Sarah said, her voice heavy with frustration. "I could see it in their faces."

Jonathan nodded. "The congregation didn't know how to handle them. They're so used to people who look and act just like them."

"But isn't that the whole point of the church?" Sarah asked. "To be a refuge for everyone? For the broken, the lost, the hurting? When did we start acting like a country club?"

Jonathan leaned back in his chair, running a hand through his hair. "I don't know. Maybe we've been like this for longer than we realized. Maybe we've just been too blind to see it."

Sarah placed her hand on his. "We need to change, Jonathan. Not just us, but the church. If we can't love people like them, then we're failing at the very thing we're called to do."

Jonathan nodded, the weight of her words sinking in. The visitors had revealed something deeply wrong in the heart of their church—and he knew it wouldn't be an easy fix. But one thing was clear: the church needed to remember what it meant to love. And it had to start now.

Chapter 4: The Prophetic Warning

The sanctuary was eerily quiet for a Wednesday evening prayer meeting. Only a handful of congregants had shown up, scattered across the pews. Pastor Jonathan sat on the edge of the pulpit, hands clasped, as Sarah led a soft, reflective hymn on the piano. He couldn't shake the unease that had been growing in his spirit since Sunday's encounter with the visitors.

Suddenly, the creak of the sanctuary door broke the stillness. A young man stepped inside, his appearance catching everyone's attention. He looked no older than twenty-five, with a rugged jacket draped over his thin frame and a leather-bound Bible clutched tightly in his hand. His dark eyes carried an intensity that made Jonathan sit up straighter.

"Can I help you?" Jonathan asked, rising from the pulpit.

The young man walked deliberately down the aisle, his footsteps echoing in the empty sanctuary. He stopped just short of the pulpit, looking directly at Jonathan.

"My name is Elijah," he said, his voice steady but filled with urgency. "I come with a message from the Lord."

A ripple of murmurs spread through the few gathered attendees. Sarah stopped playing the piano, turning her full attention to the stranger.

Jonathan stepped closer. "What kind of message?"

Elijah opened his Bible, his hands trembling slightly as he turned to Revelation 2. "The Lord says this: 'To the angel of the church in Ephesus write: These are the words of him who holds the seven stars in his right hand and walks among the seven golden lampstands. I know your deeds, your hard work and your perseverance. Yet I hold this against you: You have forsaken the love you had at first.'"

The words hung heavy in the air as Elijah looked up, his piercing gaze meeting Jonathan's. "Pastor, your church—and many others—have lost their first love. You have replaced it with rituals, pride, and the pursuit of comfort. The lampstand is in danger of being removed."

Jonathan's mouth went dry. The passage was familiar, but hearing it spoken in this context felt like a sharp rebuke.

Elijah continued, his voice growing stronger. "The Lord is calling His church to repent and return to Him. If you do not, the time of grace will end, and judgment will come before the rapture. The church is meant to be the light of the world, but your flame has grown dim. Without love, you are nothing."

The room was utterly silent. Jonathan glanced at Sarah, whose eyes were wide with a mixture of fear and awe.

"What are we supposed to do?" Jonathan asked, his voice barely above a whisper.

Elijah closed his Bible and took a deep breath. "You must lead the way. Repent, not just as individuals but as a body. Love must be restored to the heart of the church, or the world will fall further into darkness. You have a short time to act."

One of the older congregants, Mrs. Elkins, stood up, her arms crossed. "How do we know you're really sent by God? Anyone can walk in here with a Bible and call themselves a prophet."

Elijah turned to her, unflinching. "You will know by the fruit of what I say. Watch, and you will see the truth unfold. The Lord is patient, but His patience is not endless."

Mrs. Elkins sat down, her expression unsure but subdued.

Elijah turned back to Jonathan. "The church has been given a mission, Pastor. To shine as a light in the darkness, to disciple the nations, to reflect Christ's love. But you cannot fulfill that mission if you have abandoned love. Without love, your words are noise, and your works are dead."

Jonathan felt the weight of Elijah's words settle deep in his spirit. He had always thought of himself as a faithful servant, but now he wondered: Had he been serving out of duty rather than love? Had his church become more focused on preserving tradition than on truly living out the gospel?

Before Jonathan could respond, Elijah stepped back, looking toward the exit. "I have delivered the message. What you do next is up to you."

"Wait," Jonathan called. "Can you stay? Help us understand what to do?"

Elijah shook his head. "I am only a messenger. The answers you seek are in the Word and in the Spirit. Seek them earnestly."

With that, he turned and walked out, leaving the congregation in stunned silence.

After Elijah's departure, the small group erupted in whispers. Some dismissed him as an overzealous young man; others felt convicted by his words. But Jonathan sat quietly, staring at the open Bible in his lap.

Sarah placed a hand on his shoulder. "What are you thinking?"

Jonathan looked at her, his eyes filled with both fear and determination. "I think he's right. We've been so focused on everything else—attendance, programs, theology—that we've forgotten the most important thing. We've forgotten how to love."

"What do we do now?" she asked.

"We repent," Jonathan said firmly. "And then we figure out how to bring love back—not just to our church, but to every church. Before it's too late."

The weight of Elijah's words lingered, but in the midst of the conviction, Jonathan felt a spark of hope. Perhaps it wasn't too late. Perhaps the fire could be rekindled.

But one thing was clear: the road ahead would not be easy.

Chapter 5: The Lost Virtue

The room was packed with church leaders from across the city, a rare gathering of pastors, elders, and ministry heads representing denominations as diverse as their doctrines. The meeting had been called in response to the mysterious letters and the growing sense of unease within the Christian community. Everyone seemed to agree that something was wrong, but as Pastor Jonathan looked around the room, he wondered if they were ready to confront the truth.

The conference table was long, but not long enough to contain the undercurrent of tension. Bibles were stacked beside coffee cups, and a few well-worn notebooks lay open, filled with scribbled notes. Despite the signs of readiness, the atmosphere felt more like a courtroom than a gathering of God's people.

Jonathan sat near the middle of the table, with Sarah at his side. Across from him was Pastor Clark, a firebrand preacher from a Pentecostal church. Next to him sat Father Martinez, a soft-spoken Catholic priest. Further down, Reverend Harris, an elder statesman of the Methodist tradition, adjusted his glasses and cleared his throat, signaling his impatience.

The meeting began with a prayer, but the moment the "Amen" was spoken, the arguments began.

"We're here because the church has lost its way," Jonathan started, addressing the group. "The letter and the words of Revelation 2:4-5 aren't just a warning—they're a wake-up call. If we don't restore love, if we don't rediscover the heart of Christ, we risk losing everything."

Pastor Clark leaned forward, his voice booming. "You're talking about love like it's some fluffy concept, Pastor. The problem isn't a lack of love—it's a lack of holiness! The church has become too soft on sin. We need to preach repentance, fire, and brimstone."

Father Martinez frowned. "While I agree repentance is essential, love is not secondary. Christ's ministry began and ended with love. Without it, holiness is just legalism."

"And what does 'love' even mean anymore?" Reverend Harris interjected. "Is it about tolerance? Accepting everyone no matter what they do? That's the kind of message that's watered down the gospel."

The room erupted into a cacophony of voices. Some nodded in agreement with Reverend Harris, while others shook their heads vehemently. Sarah looked at Jonathan, her expression tense, as the meeting spiraled into theological squabbling.

A woman named Deaconess Ruth, representing a small evangelical church, finally stood and raised her hands. "Brothers and sisters, please! We're not here to argue about doctrine. We're here to find solutions. People are hurting. The world is falling apart, and we're too busy fighting each other to help them."

Her words quieted the room, but only for a moment.

"We need to address doctrine, Deaconess," Pastor Clark insisted. "Without sound teaching, how can we lead? This isn't about emotions—it's about truth."

Jonathan felt his frustration rising. "And what is truth without love, Pastor Clark? Paul himself said, 'If I speak in the tongues of men and of angels but do not have love, I am only a resounding gong or a clanging cymbal.'" He looked around the room. "We can't keep doing this—splitting hairs over theology while people are leaving the church in droves."

"You want unity? Fine," Reverend Harris snapped. "But don't expect my church to compromise its values to fit some feel-good agenda."

Father Martinez sighed deeply. "No one is asking for compromise. We're being asked to remember why we are here—to reflect the love of Christ."

Hours passed, but the meeting produced no real progress. Every proposal was met with resistance, and every attempt to unify was thwarted by entrenched divisions. As the arguments continued, Jonathan felt a deep sadness settle over him. It was clear that the problem ran deeper than he had imagined. The church wasn't just missing love—it was missing humility, selflessness, and a willingness to listen.

Finally, Deaconess Ruth stood again, her voice trembling. "If we can't come together to restore love in the church, then what hope does the world have? We're supposed to be the light, but we're standing here arguing while the darkness spreads."

Her words hung in the air, but the silence that followed wasn't one of agreement. It was one of resignation. One by one, the leaders began to leave, their faces etched with frustration and fatigue.

As the room emptied, Jonathan and Sarah sat in their chairs, feeling defeated.

"I thought we could come together," Jonathan said, staring at the now-empty table. "I thought if we worked together, we could make a difference."

Sarah placed a hand on his arm. "They're scared, Jonathan. Scared of losing control, scared of being wrong. It's hard to lead with love when fear is driving you."

Jonathan nodded slowly. "But we can't give up. If they won't act, then we will. Somehow, we have to find a way to show them that love isn't just a concept—it's the very foundation of our faith."

Sarah smiled faintly. "We'll start with us. Maybe if they see love in action, they'll remember what it looks like."

Jonathan took a deep breath, feeling the weight of the task ahead. The meeting had ended in failure, but he wasn't ready to give up. Somewhere, deep within the fractured church, the flame of love was still flickering. And he was determined to fan it into a blaze.

Chapter 6: The Investigators

The sunlight streamed through the stained-glass windows of the small conference room in the church, casting multicolored patterns across the walls. It was a stark contrast to the serious atmosphere inside. Pastor Jonathan sat at the head of the table, a Bible open in front of him, flanked by Sarah, who quietly poured coffee for the group.

Around the table sat six individuals, each representing a different Christian tradition. They had all agreed—sometimes reluctantly—to join the team that Jonathan and Sarah were forming to investigate what had gone wrong in the global church. The mission was clear: to uncover why love had disappeared and how it could be restored.

The Team

1. **Deaconess Ruth** - The fiery evangelical leader whose bold faith and practical wisdom made her a natural choice.
2. **Father Martinez** - The soft-spoken Catholic priest, who carried a calm presence but often acted as the mediator in heated discussions.
3. **Pastor Clark** - A zealous Pentecostal with a passion for holiness but a tendency toward strong opinions.
4. **Reverend Harris** - The Methodist elder with years of experience but a guarded stance on ecumenical efforts.
5. **Kayla Washington** - A young non-denominational worship leader, known for her empathy and fresh perspective.
6. **Elder Samuel** - A Baptist lay minister, whose quiet demeanor often belied his deep understanding of Scripture.

Each of them came from a different tradition, with unique theological views and approaches to ministry. The differences were immediately apparent, but so was the underlying sense that they all recognized the seriousness of the task before them.

Jonathan began the meeting with a prayer, asking for wisdom and unity. When he finished, he looked around the table. "Thank you all for being here. I know we don't all agree on everything, but this isn't about our differences. It's about something we all share—faith in Jesus Christ and the knowledge that something vital is missing from His church."

Pastor Clark was the first to speak. "I'm here because I agree that something needs to change. But I'm telling you now, this isn't just about 'love.' The problem is that the church has compromised too much with the world. We've lost our standards."

Kayla raised an eyebrow. "With respect, Pastor, how can we call ourselves followers of Christ if we're more concerned about rules than loving people? Love is the standard."

Reverend Harris sighed, leaning back in his chair. "This is exactly what I was afraid of. Everyone has a different definition of what love means. How are we supposed to fix something we can't even agree on?"

Deaconess Ruth slammed her hand on the table. "Enough. Love isn't up for debate. Scripture is clear: 'By this everyone will know that you are my disciples, if you love one another.' That's what Jesus said. So let's stop arguing and start figuring out how we lost sight of it."

The room fell silent. Jonathan nodded, grateful for Ruth's directness. "She's right. We're not here to defend our traditions or doctrines. We're here to investigate. What happened to love in the church? Why has it disappeared, and how can we bring it back?"

The First Steps

Father Martinez spoke next, his voice calm but firm. "If we are to investigate, we must start with humility. The church is the Bride of Christ, but she has grown divided. Our first step should be to examine ourselves and our own hearts before we look outward."

Sarah added, "And we need to look at history. When did things start to change? Was there a moment when love began to fade, or has it been a gradual decline?"

Elder Samuel nodded. "The Bible is clear that love is the greatest of all virtues. But it also warns that in the last days, 'the love of many will grow cold.' Maybe we're seeing that prophecy come to pass."

Pastor Clark frowned. "If that's the case, are we wasting our time? If this is part of God's plan for the end times, what can we do?"

Kayla leaned forward. "God's plan doesn't give us permission to give up. We're called to love no matter what. If the church is failing, then we have to figure out how to be the spark that reignites it."

Jonathan felt a surge of hope as he listened. Despite their differences, there was a shared determination in the room. "We'll start by gathering information," he said. "Talking to other churches, studying Scripture, and looking at how the church has changed over the years. And we'll pray—constantly. This isn't just a human effort. If we're going to find what's missing, we need God to guide us."

The Commitment

By the end of the meeting, each member of the team had committed to the mission. They knew it wouldn't be easy. Their differences would challenge them, and the task before them seemed impossible. But they also knew they couldn't ignore the call. Love was missing, and the church couldn't survive without it.

As the group dispersed, Sarah turned to Jonathan. "Do you think they'll stick with it?"

Jonathan smiled faintly. "They're here, aren't they? That's a start. And I think God has brought us together for a reason."

In the days ahead, the team would face conflicts, revelations, and spiritual battles. But for now, they had taken the first step: a commitment to find the missing virtue that the church—and the world—desperately needed.

Love.

Part 2: The Search for Love

Chapter 7: The First Clue

The conference room was quiet except for the occasional rustle of Bible pages. The team had gathered again, this time with a single focus: uncovering what the cryptic warning in Revelation 2:4-5 truly meant for the church today. Pastor Jonathan stood at the whiteboard, the verse written in bold letters behind him:

> "Yet I hold this against you: You have forsaken the love you had at first. Consider how far you have fallen! Repent and do the things you did at first. If you do not repent, I will come to you and remove your lampstand from its place."

Jonathan underlined the phrase *"the love you had at first"* and turned to the team. "This is where it all begins. The letter to the church in Ephesus isn't just a rebuke—it's a roadmap. If we can understand what this love is, we can begin to find our way back."

Dissecting the Text

Father Martinez leaned forward, his Bible open on the table. "The love mentioned here isn't just about feelings. It's the agape love of God—a selfless, sacrificial love that reflects Christ's heart. The Ephesians were praised for their deeds and perseverance, but they were rebuked for losing that love."

Deaconess Ruth nodded. "They were still doing good works, but their motivation had shifted. Without love, all their actions were hollow."

Reverend Harris adjusted his glasses. "So, we're looking at a spiritual problem, not just a behavioral one. The church has become more focused on appearances, programs, and traditions than on the heart of the gospel."

Kayla chimed in, her voice thoughtful. "But it's not just about the church as an institution. This applies to us, too. How often do we go through the motions—attending services, volunteering—without really loving God or others?"

Pastor Clark frowned. "True. But how do we 'restore' this love? It's not like flipping a switch."

Sarah stood and walked to the whiteboard, taking a marker. "Look at what it says next: *'Consider how far you have fallen! Repent and do the things you did at first.'* The answer is in those three steps—remember, repent, and return."

Step 1: Remember

Sarah drew a circle on the board. "First, we have to remember. What did the church look like when it was full of love? What did it feel like to truly experience God's love in our lives? Before we can restore love, we need to remember what we've lost."

Elder Samuel spoke up, his voice measured. "In the early church, love was evident in how they cared for one another. Acts 2:44-47 talks about believers sharing everything, meeting each other's needs, and worshiping together with glad hearts. That kind of love wasn't just an emotion—it was action."

Father Martinez nodded. "And it was rooted in their devotion to Christ. They didn't just love each other—they loved God with all their heart, soul, and mind."

Step 2: Repent

Sarah wrote the word *Repent* inside the circle. "The next step is repentance. That means acknowledging where we've gone wrong—both as individuals and as the church."

Pastor Clark crossed his arms. "Repentance isn't easy. It means admitting that we've let pride, selfishness, and complacency take over. And it means turning away from those things."

Kayla added, "It's not just about saying 'sorry.' True repentance means changing direction. It's about realigning our hearts with God's."

Step 3: Return

Sarah finished the circle with the word *Return.* "Finally, we have to go back to the basics—doing the things we did at first. That means loving God passionately and loving others selflessly. It means discipleship, service, and being the hands and feet of Christ."

Jonathan stepped forward, his expression serious. "This is more than just a checklist. If we're going to restore love in the church, it has to start with us. We have to live it out in a way that's contagious."

Connecting the Rapture

Elder Samuel, who had been quiet for most of the meeting, spoke up. "I've been thinking about how this ties into the rapture. The church is the Bride of Christ. If we're called to be ready for His return, how can we be ready if we're not walking in love?"

Reverend Harris nodded. "The lampstand represents the church's witness. If we don't restore love, our witness is dead—and without a witness, we're not fulfilling the Great Commission."

Kayla's eyes widened. "So, this isn't just about us. The world is spiraling because the church isn't shining its light. If we don't restore love, we're not just failing ourselves—we're failing the world."

The First Clue

Jonathan picked up his Bible and turned to Revelation 2 again. "The warning to Ephesus wasn't about losing salvation—it was about losing their place as a light in the world. The rapture is coming, but we have a job to do before then. If the church can't restore love, we're leaving the world in chaos."

Sarah added, "And if we can restore it, we won't just prepare ourselves for Christ's return—we'll bring hope to a world that desperately needs it."

The team sat in silence for a moment, the weight of the task before them sinking in.

Jonathan finally broke the silence. "We've found our first clue. Love isn't just something we've lost—it's something we have to fight to restore. And it starts with us. From this point forward, we live it, we teach it, and we spread it. No matter how hard it gets."

The team nodded in agreement, a sense of purpose filling the room. They had taken their first step toward uncovering the truth—and rekindling the flame that had grown dim in the church.

The journey had begun.

Chapter 8: Revisiting the Past

The team gathered in the fellowship hall of a nearby church, a modest space with faded linoleum floors and folding chairs. A small group of elders sat in a semicircle, their weathered faces reflecting years of faith and service. These men and women had lived through seasons when the church was vibrant, overflowing with love and discipleship. Now, they had been invited to share their memories, offering a glimpse into what the church had once been.

Jonathan stood at the front of the room, clipboard in hand. "Thank you all for being here. We're trying to understand what the church used to look like when it was full of love—when discipleship wasn't just a program but a way of life. Your memories are invaluable."

The Early Days

Mrs. Beatrice, a spry woman in her eighties, was the first to speak. Her voice trembled slightly, but her eyes sparkled with conviction. "I remember the days when the church wasn't just a building—it was a family. We shared meals, prayed together, and cared for each other like kin. If someone was in need, the whole congregation rallied around them."

Father Martinez nodded. "That sounds like the church described in Acts."

Beatrice smiled. "It was. I remember when Pastor Henry used to visit every home in the community, whether they were members or not. He said, 'You can't love people from a distance.' That's how we grew—not through big events, but through simple acts of love."

Discipleship as a Lifestyle

Elder James, a retired deacon, leaned forward. "Back then, discipleship wasn't something we scheduled once a week. It was a way of life. Older believers mentored younger ones, teaching them how to pray, study the Bible, and live out their faith. It wasn't flashy, but it was real."

Kayla jotted down notes, her brow furrowed. "What changed?"

James sighed. "We got busy. People stopped making time for each other. The church started focusing more on programs and less on relationships. Before we knew it, discipleship became an afterthought."

A Heart for the Lost

Mr. Louis, a soft-spoken elder with a cane, chimed in. "The church used to have a real heart for the lost. We didn't wait for people to come to us—we went to them. I remember walking the streets, knocking on doors, sharing the gospel with anyone who would listen. And we did it because we loved them, not because we wanted to fill pews."

Pastor Clark's expression softened. "It sounds like the church wasn't just preaching love—it was living it."

Louis nodded. "Exactly. Love wasn't just a sermon topic. It was the way we lived."

The Turning Point

Sarah leaned forward. "When did things start to change?"

The room grew quiet. Finally, Mrs. Beatrice spoke again. "I think it was gradual. At some point, we started focusing more on numbers—attendance, budgets, programs. We wanted to grow, but in doing so, we lost sight of why we were growing. The love we had for God and each other was replaced by goals and strategies."

Reverend Harris folded his arms. "It sounds like the church became more about appearances than substance."

Elder James nodded. "We stopped teaching the younger generation how to love and serve. We assumed they'd pick it up by watching us, but they didn't. Now, we have churches full of people who don't know what it means to truly follow Christ."

The Lessons Learned

Jonathan stepped forward, addressing the elders. "If you could go back and do one thing differently, what would it be?"

Mrs. Beatrice's eyes filled with tears. "I would remind everyone to keep Jesus at the center. When you truly love Him, that love spills over into everything else—your relationships, your service, your worship. We forgot that. We let other things take His place."

Louis added, "I'd say the same. Love isn't something you can manufacture. It has to come from God. If we don't stay connected to Him, we lose everything."

Jonathan's voice softened. "Thank you. Your insights have given us a lot to think about."

Reflection

As the meeting ended, the team gathered in a corner to debrief.

"They're right," Kayla said, her voice heavy with emotion. "We've traded relationships for programs. Love can't thrive in that kind of environment."

Pastor Clark, uncharacteristically subdued, nodded. "We've been so focused on results that we've forgotten the basics. No wonder love is missing."

Jonathan took a deep breath. "We've found another piece of the puzzle. Love isn't just an abstract idea—it's something that has to be lived out in real, tangible ways. And it starts with going back to what the church used to do: building relationships, discipling intentionally, and keeping Christ at the center."

Sarah placed a hand on his shoulder. "We've got a lot of work to do."

Jonathan smiled faintly. "We do. But at least now, we know where to start."

As the team left the church, the elders' words echoed in their hearts. The road ahead was long, but they were beginning to see a path forward—a path paved with love, humility, and a renewed commitment to the mission of Christ.

Chapter 9: The Hardened Hearts

It was a bright Sunday morning, but the atmosphere inside Grace Community Church was anything but welcoming. The pews were nearly full, a rare sight in recent weeks. Word had spread that Pastor Jonathan had been preaching on love and repentance, and curiosity had drawn a larger crowd.

Among the attendees were several new faces—visitors who didn't quite fit the mold of the usual congregation. A group of young adults with tattoos and piercings sat near the back, whispering among themselves. A middle-aged man in a tattered jacket, likely homeless, had taken a seat near the aisle. Two young women, their attire more suited for a nightclub than a church, sat nervously in the corner.

Jonathan noticed the tension immediately. The congregation's polite smiles were strained, and their whispered conversations carried an unmistakable undertone of judgment.

The Brewing Storm

As the service began, the worship team struggled to lead the congregation. The songs, meant to stir hearts and bring unity, fell flat. Eyes darted toward the newcomers, who stood awkwardly during the hymns. A few members deliberately avoided them, shifting to seats further away.

Jonathan stepped up to the pulpit, his prepared sermon feeling heavier than usual. He glanced at the visitors, then at his congregation. *Lord, help me speak your truth with love,* he prayed silently.

His sermon focused on Matthew 22:37-39: *"Love the Lord your God with all your heart and with all your soul and with all your mind... And love your neighbor as yourself."*

"As Christians, we are called to love—radically, unconditionally, just as Christ loves us," Jonathan preached. "But love isn't just words. It's action. It's how we treat the least of these, the broken, the outcasts."

He paused, scanning the room. Some nodded in agreement, but others shifted uncomfortably in their seats. The visitors, meanwhile, sat motionless, their expressions guarded.

The Breaking Point

After the sermon, the congregation moved into a time of prayer. Jonathan encouraged everyone to pray for one another, inviting the visitors to join small groups for personal prayer. That's when it happened.

One of the visitors—a young man with brightly dyed hair and a chain necklace—stood to approach a prayer circle. Before he could speak, an older deacon named Mr. Fields stepped in front of him, blocking his path.

"Son," Mr. Fields said, his voice low but firm, "this is a house of God. We expect a certain level of respect here. Perhaps you should reconsider how you present yourself before coming back."

The room fell silent. The young man's face flushed with anger and humiliation. "I came here looking for peace," he said, his voice shaking. "I didn't know I had to pass some kind of test to pray."

Mr. Fields opened his mouth to respond, but before he could, one of the young man's friends stood up. "This is why people don't come to church!" she shouted, her voice cracking. "You talk about love, but you don't mean it."

The tension exploded. Voices rose, accusations flew, and members of the congregation began to argue—not just with the visitors, but with one another.

"Why are we letting people like this in here?" one woman hissed.
"They're children of God, just like us!" another countered.
"If they want to be here, they should respect our standards."
"Standards? What about grace?"

The young man, overwhelmed, turned and started for the door. "Forget this," he muttered. His friends followed, leaving the sanctuary in chaos.

Jonathan's Heartbreak

Jonathan stepped forward, raising his hands in an attempt to calm the crowd. "Stop!" he shouted, his voice trembling with frustration. "What are we doing? This is God's house, and we're driving people away!"

The room quieted, but the damage was done. Jonathan's words echoed in the silence: "We just proved we don't understand the love of Christ."

A Painful Aftermath

After the service, Jonathan sat in his office with Sarah, his head in his hands. "I've failed," he said, his voice hollow. "I preached about love, and we ended up doing the exact opposite."

Sarah placed a hand on his shoulder. "This isn't just about you, Jonathan. It's about all of us. The church has hardened its heart for so long, it's forgotten how to love."

Deaconess Ruth entered, her face grim. "I've seen disagreements in the church before, but never anything like this. It's like the very mention of love sets people off."

Jonathan looked up at her, his eyes filled with determination. "Then we need to confront it. The church has hardened its heart, but hearts can change. We have to believe that."

Reflection

Later that evening, the team met to debrief. The events of the day weighed heavily on them all.

Father Martinez spoke first. "What happened today was painful, but it revealed the truth. We've been so focused on outward appearances and traditions that we've neglected the heart of the gospel."

Kayla added, "It's not just about teaching love. It's about modeling it. If the congregation doesn't see it in us, how can we expect them to live it out?"

Pastor Clark, usually defensive, nodded solemnly. "I saw myself in Mr. Fields today. I've been so focused on correcting others that I've forgotten to show grace. We have a lot of work to do."

Jonathan leaned forward, his voice steady. "What happened today was a wake-up call. We have to lead by example, even when it's uncomfortable. Love isn't easy, but it's the only way forward."

As the meeting ended, the team left with a renewed sense of purpose. The events of the day had exposed the church's hardened heart, but they also revealed an opportunity—a chance to rebuild on a foundation of true, Christ-like love.

Chapter 10: A Journey Through Denominations

The team set out on their journey, each carrying a notebook and a heavy heart. Their mission was simple but daunting: visit churches from different denominations, observe, and uncover what had replaced love in these sacred spaces. What they found would both grieve and challenge them.

The Stiff Walls of Legalism

Their first stop was a conservative Baptist church nestled in a quiet suburban neighborhood. The sanctuary was pristine, with polished wooden pews and neatly arranged hymnals. The service was structured and orderly, each moment carefully planned.

During the sermon, the pastor spoke with precision, expounding on doctrine with fervor. Yet, as the team watched, they noticed the lack of warmth among the congregation. People sat stoically, nodding occasionally but never engaging beyond the surface.

After the service, Sarah approached a group of congregants. "It's wonderful to see so many people committed to the Word," she said, smiling.

One woman nodded stiffly. "We believe in holding firm to the truth. Compromising on doctrine is why the church is in decline."

Kayla, standing nearby, ventured, "But how do you show love to those who don't yet know the truth?"

The woman frowned. "Love comes through obedience. If people don't follow God's commands, they have no place here."

As they left the church, Father Martinez sighed. "The truth is important, but without love, it becomes a weapon rather than a guide."

The Fog of Complacency

Their next visit took them to a large, modern non-denominational church. The sanctuary resembled a theater, complete with stage lights and a professional sound system. The worship team performed with energy, and the pastor delivered an inspiring message filled with motivational quotes.

At first, the team was encouraged by the lively atmosphere. But as they spoke to members after the service, a troubling pattern emerged.

"We love coming here," one young couple said. "The sermons are so positive, and we always leave feeling good."

Jonathan pressed gently. "How does this church help you grow spiritually?"

The couple exchanged uncertain looks. "Well, we don't really get involved much. We just attend on Sundays. It's all we need."

Deaconess Ruth shook her head as they walked to the car. "They're being fed milk when they need meat. Without discipleship and accountability, love becomes shallow—just a feel-good experience."

The Poison of Division

Their third stop was a small Pentecostal church in a rural community. The congregation was vibrant, their worship passionate. People danced, clapped, and shouted praises, their enthusiasm filling the room.

But during the fellowship hour, cracks began to show. A group of older members huddled in a corner, whispering about the new pastor's changes. Younger members spoke about feeling judged for their choices. The division was palpable.

One young woman confided in Kayla, "I used to love this church, but it feels like we're always fighting. Half the congregation thinks we're too traditional, and the other half thinks we're too modern."

Reverend Harris sighed. "Unity doesn't mean uniformity, but without love, even the smallest differences can tear us apart."

A Moment of Reflection

The team gathered that evening in a small café, sharing their observations.

"We've seen three very different churches," Jonathan began, "but the problem is the same. Love has been replaced by legalism, complacency, or division."

Deaconess Ruth nodded. "Legalism focuses on rules at the expense of relationships. Complacency avoids conflict but fails to challenge people to grow. And division destroys unity, making love impossible."

Pastor Clark, who had been unusually quiet, spoke up. "I've been guilty of some of these things myself. I've pushed for holiness without considering how to love the people I'm correcting."

Kayla added, "It's like every church has forgotten that love isn't just one part of the gospel—it *is* the gospel. Without it, nothing else matters."

Father Martinez leaned forward. "Paul said it best in 1 Corinthians 13: 'If I have a faith that can move mountains, but do not have love, I am nothing.' These churches are doing good things—teaching doctrine, worshiping, serving—but they've lost the heart behind it all."

Hope for Change

Jonathan closed his notebook. "We have a long way to go, but today was eye-opening. These churches aren't beyond hope—they just need to remember why they exist. It's not to preserve traditions or entertain people or win theological debates. It's to love God and love others."

Sarah smiled. "And maybe if we can show them what that looks like, they'll start to believe it's possible."

As the team left the café, they carried with them a renewed sense of purpose. The journey through denominations had revealed the depth of the problem, but it had also given them clarity: the church's greatest need was not better programs or stricter rules—it was the radical, life-changing love of Christ. And their mission was to reignite that flame.

Chapter 11: The Mirror of the World

The team sat in the dimly lit living room of Pastor Jonathan's home, the weight of their recent experiences heavy on their shoulders. The air was thick with contemplation as they recounted their visits to various churches. Each notebook was filled with observations—some hopeful, but most alarming.

Sarah set down her tea and broke the silence. "It's like every church we visited is stuck in survival mode—focused on their own needs, their own traditions, their own fears. And meanwhile, the world is falling apart."

Elder Samuel nodded. "It's no coincidence. The church is supposed to be the light of the world, but if we're not shining, darkness is bound to spread."

The Evidence of Decay

Jonathan pulled out his laptop and began scrolling through headlines, his frustration evident. He read aloud:

- *"Violent Crime at All-Time High"*
- *"Global Leaders Admit Failure to Address Poverty"*
- *"Families Torn Apart by Addiction and Depression"*

"These headlines aren't just news stories—they're symptoms," he said. "Symptoms of a world without a moral compass, without hope. And the church is supposed to be the solution, but we've been too busy arguing and isolating ourselves to notice."

Deaconess Ruth leaned forward. "We've let the world outpace us in addressing human need. Governments and charities are trying, but they can't provide the one thing that truly changes lives: the love of Christ."

Kayla added, "And when the church fails to model that love, the world has nothing to look up to. We've become a reflection of the world instead of a mirror of God's love."

The Church's Impact—or Lack Thereof

Pastor Clark, usually vocal, had been uncharacteristically quiet. He finally spoke, his tone somber. "I've spent years preaching about holiness and calling out sin in the world. But today I'm realizing that we've failed at something even more important: loving the world as Christ does."

Father Martinez nodded. "When Jesus looked at the crowds, He was moved with compassion, not condemnation. But we've traded compassion for judgment, and the world has noticed. They don't see us as a refuge anymore—they see us as their accusers."

Reverend Harris sighed. "It's no wonder people are leaving the church. Why would they come to us when all they find is criticism or indifference?"

Sarah interjected, "But it's not just about people leaving the church. It's about the void we've left in the world. If we're not leading with love, someone else will step in—and they won't lead toward Christ."

A Harsh Realization

Jonathan stood and paced the room. "Think about it. When the church thrived in love, we saw revivals, social reform, and families strengthened. But now, we're divided and distracted, and the world has followed suit."

Deaconess Ruth nodded solemnly. "The church is supposed to be the salt of the earth. Salt preserves, but it also seasons—it adds flavor. Without us, the world has grown stale and corrupt. And Jesus warned what happens when salt loses its flavor: it's thrown out and trampled underfoot."

Father Martinez quoted softly, "*'Judgment begins with the house of God.'* Maybe the chaos in the world is a reflection of our failure as the church. If we had been living out love, discipling intentionally, and being the light, would the world look this way?"

The room fell silent. The truth was painful but undeniable.

A Call to Action

Kayla broke the silence. "So, what do we do? We can't change the past, but we can start changing the present. We've seen what's wrong—now we need to be part of the solution."

Jonathan stopped pacing and turned to the group. "We need to remind the church—and ourselves—that our mission is bigger than maintaining traditions or preaching from a pulpit. It's about showing the world what love looks like. Real love. Sacrificial, selfless, Christ-like love."

Sarah added, "And that starts with us. We can't ask the church to change if we're not willing to live it out first."

The Mirror of the World

The team began to see the world's brokenness not as a separate issue, but as a mirror reflecting the church's own failures. The moral decay, the division, the despair—all of it pointed back to the absence of love within the Body of Christ.

But they also saw hope. If the church could reclaim its first love, if believers could truly live as Christ intended, the ripple effect could transform not just the church, but the world.

Jonathan closed the meeting with a prayer: "Lord, forgive us for where we've fallen short. Help us to love as You love, to shine as Your light, and to bring hope to a world in desperate need of You. Show us how to lead the way back to Your heart. Amen."

The team left that night with a renewed determination. They had seen the darkness, but they also knew the source of the light. Their mission was clear: to reignite love within the church so it could once again be a beacon of hope for the world.

Chapter 12: The Prayer Revival

The team gathered in the small chapel of Father Martinez's church, a humble but sacred space lit by the flicker of candles. The wooden pews creaked softly as they sat together, their Bibles open but untouched. Tonight, their mission wasn't about studying Scripture or analyzing the state of the church—it was about prayer.

The tension in the room was palpable. Though they had worked together for weeks, the differences among them still lingered like an invisible wall. Pastor Clark's firm Pentecostal beliefs often clashed with Reverend Harris's measured Methodist approach. Deaconess Ruth's boldness sometimes overshadowed Kayla's softer, contemplative spirit. Even Father Martinez's calm demeanor occasionally stirred unease in Elder Samuel, who was wary of Catholic traditions.

Jonathan stood at the front of the room, his hands clasped in front of him. "We've seen the problem," he began, his voice steady. "We've studied Scripture, visited churches, and talked to people. But tonight, it's time to set aside everything else and go straight to the source. If we're going to restore love in the church, we need to start on our knees."

Setting Aside Differences

The team knelt together at the altar, a mix of postures reflecting their varied traditions. Some clasped their hands tightly, others lifted them toward heaven, while a few simply bowed their heads. It was a visible reminder of their diversity—but also of their shared faith.

"Let's pray openly," Sarah suggested, her voice soft but firm. "Whatever is on your heart, lift it up. This isn't about denominations or theology. It's about seeking God together."

Kayla was the first to speak. "Lord, I confess that I've been hesitant—afraid to speak boldly about love because I didn't want to offend anyone. Forgive me for holding back when the world needs Your truth. Teach me to love with courage."

Elder Samuel followed. "Father, I've been prideful. I've judged others for their traditions and focused more on being right than on being loving. Forgive me, and help me see my brothers and sisters the way You do."

One by one, the team confessed their fears, frustrations, and shortcomings. Pastor Clark, his voice trembling, admitted, "God, I've been so focused on calling out sin that I've forgotten to show grace. Forgive me for the times I've pushed people away instead of drawing them closer to You."

Father Martinez prayed next, his words calm but heartfelt. "Lord, unite us in Your Spirit. Break down the walls we've built between us—walls of pride, misunderstanding, and fear. Let us be one, as You and the Father are one."

The Breakthrough

As the prayers continued, the atmosphere in the room began to shift. What had started as a collection of individual prayers became a unified cry for help. Their voices overlapped, rising and falling in a symphony of desperation and hope.

Kayla began to sing softly, a familiar worship song:
"Spirit of the living God, fall afresh on me..."

The others joined in, their voices hesitant at first but growing stronger with each verse. The melody filled the chapel, weaving through the cracks in their hearts and binding them together in a way words never could.

Jonathan lifted his hands, tears streaming down his face. "Lord, we surrender. We don't have the answers, but You do. Teach us to love as You love. Show us how to bring Your light into this broken world."

At that moment, a deep sense of peace descended upon the room. The tension that had divided them melted away, replaced by a profound awareness of God's presence. It was as though the walls they had built around their hearts had been torn down, leaving only humility and a shared longing for God's love to be restored.

A Vision of Unity

As they prayed, Kayla suddenly gasped, her hands clutching her chest. "I see something," she whispered, her voice trembling. "It's... a flame. It's small, almost out, but it's starting to grow. It's flickering brighter... and it's spreading."

Pastor Clark's eyes widened. "The fire of the Spirit."

Kayla nodded, tears streaming down her face. "It's not just one flame—it's thousands, lighting up all over the world. But it starts here. It starts with us."

The team sat in stunned silence, the weight of the vision sinking in. Jonathan finally spoke, his voice steady but filled with awe. "If the church is going to shine again, it has to start with the fire of God's love. And that fire begins in prayer."

The Aftermath

The team remained in the chapel long after the prayer ended, basking in the peace and unity they had found. When they finally rose to leave, their faces reflected a quiet determination.

"We've been trying to fix this on our own," Sarah said. "But tonight proved something: We can't restore love without God. It's His love, not ours, that changes hearts."

Father Martinez nodded. "And now we've seen what's possible when we pray together. If we can set aside our differences and seek God as one, the church can, too."

Jonathan looked around the room, his heart swelling with hope. "This is just the beginning. Tonight, we've seen a glimpse of what the church can be. Now, it's time to take this fire and spread it."

As they stepped out into the cool night air, the team knew they had experienced something extraordinary. The barriers between them had been broken, replaced by a bond forged in prayer. And in that moment, they realized they weren't just a team anymore—they were a family, united by their shared mission to rekindle the lost flame of love.

Chapter 13: The Missing Ingredient

The team gathered in Pastor Jonathan's study, its bookshelves lined with well-worn commentaries and Bibles. The room was cozy, with a fire crackling in the hearth and a long oak table in the center. It was a rare moment of stillness after the intensity of their journey so far.

Tonight's focus was clear: a Bible study to uncover the missing ingredient in the church's discipleship. They had prayed for guidance and unity, and now it was time to dig into Scripture to understand why love was so critical—and why its absence had left the church hollow.

The Study Begins

Sarah opened the session with a question. "We've seen churches that teach the Word, lead worship, and serve their communities, but something is still missing. Why does it feel like discipleship is incomplete?"

Deaconess Ruth flipped through her Bible, landing on a familiar passage. "Let's start with John 13:34-35," she said, reading aloud:
'A new command I give you: Love one another. As I have loved you, so you must love one another. By this everyone will know that you are my disciples, if you love one another.'

She looked up, her voice steady. "Jesus didn't say people would recognize us by our doctrine, our programs, or our traditions. He said they'd know us by our love."

Father Martinez nodded. "Love isn't just an aspect of discipleship—it's the foundation. Without it, everything else falls apart."

The Fruit of the Spirit

Kayla turned to Galatians 5:22-23 and read aloud:
'But the fruit of the Spirit is love, joy, peace, forbearance, kindness, goodness, faithfulness, gentleness, and self-control.'

She paused, tracing her finger over the page. "Notice something? Love is listed first. It's the root of all the other fruits. Without love, how can we have true joy, peace, or kindness?"

Pastor Clark leaned back in his chair, stroking his chin. "I've preached about the fruit of the Spirit for years, but I never really thought about how love holds it all together. If we're not bearing the fruit of love, then we're not walking in the Spirit."

Jonathan added, "And if we're not walking in the Spirit, our discipleship becomes mechanical—just going through the motions."

The Missing Ingredient

Elder Samuel spoke next, turning to 1 Corinthians 13:1-3:
'If I speak in the tongues of men or of angels, but do not have love, I am only a resounding gong or a clanging cymbal. If I have the gift of prophecy and can fathom all mysteries and all knowledge, and if I have a faith that can move mountains, but do not have love, I am nothing. If I give all I possess to the poor and give over my body to hardship that I may boast, but do not have love, I gain nothing.'

He looked around the room, his voice low but firm. "Paul isn't just saying that love is important—he's saying it's essential.

Without love, even the most extraordinary acts of faith and service mean nothing."

Reverend Harris sighed deeply. "It's sobering, isn't it? We've built entire ministries around teaching, prophecy, and service, but if love isn't at the center, it's all for show."

Jonathan nodded. "And that's the problem. We've been focusing on what we *do* rather than who we *are* in Christ. Discipleship isn't about producing good works—it's about producing love."

Rediscovering Love

The group grew quiet as they reflected on the passages. Finally, Kayla spoke. "So, if love is the foundation of discipleship, how do we rediscover it? How do we teach people to love when it feels like the church has forgotten how?"

Deaconess Ruth smiled faintly. "We start by looking at Jesus. His entire ministry was a demonstration of love. He loved the outcasts, the sinners, and even His enemies. If we want to restore love, we have to model our lives after His."

Father Martinez added, "And we can't forget the Holy Spirit. Romans 5:5 says, *'God's love has been poured out into our hearts through the Holy Spirit.'* Love isn't something we can manufacture—it's something God gives us when we surrender to Him."

Love in Action

Jonathan stood and wrote on the whiteboard:

- **Love God**: With all your heart, soul, and mind.
- **Love Others**: As yourself, unconditionally and sacrificially.
- **Make Disciples**: By teaching them to walk in love through Christ.

He turned to the team. "This is our mission. We've been looking for a missing ingredient, and now we've found it. Discipleship without love isn't discipleship at all."

Pastor Clark, for once, looked humbled. "You're right. I've been so focused on teaching truth that I've forgotten to teach love. And the truth is, they can't be separated."

A Call to Action

As the study ended, Sarah led the group in prayer. "Lord, thank You for revealing Your truth to us tonight. Teach us to love as You love. Let everything we do flow from Your Spirit and reflect Your heart. Help us to be disciples who make disciples, all rooted in Your love. Amen."

As they left Jonathan's study, the team felt a renewed sense of clarity and purpose. They now understood the missing ingredient in the church's discipleship and why its absence had caused so much harm. The journey ahead would still be challenging, but they had a foundation to build upon—and it was strong, unshakable, and eternal: the love of Christ.

Chapter 14: The Battle Within

The prayer and Bible study had been a breakthrough, but the journey was far from over. The deeper the team delved into their mission to restore love to the church, the more their own weaknesses began to surface. It was as though the closer they came to the truth, the more their flaws were exposed. Each member carried hidden struggles, unspoken frustrations, and buried pride—and now, those cracks were beginning to show.

Tensions Rise

It started with something small during one of their meetings. Deaconess Ruth and Pastor Clark were discussing the team's next steps, but the conversation quickly turned into a heated debate.

"We need to focus on the Word," Pastor Clark insisted, his voice rising. "That's the foundation of everything. Without solid teaching, all this talk about love is meaningless."

Ruth folded her arms, her tone sharp. "And what good is teaching if it's not lived out? The Word is important, but people need to see love in action."

Father Martinez tried to mediate. "Both points are valid. Perhaps we can—"

Pastor Clark cut him off. "With respect, Father, your traditions focus more on rituals than Scripture. Maybe that's part of the problem."

The room fell silent. Father Martinez's face flushed, but he stayed composed. "And perhaps," he said calmly, "we should consider whether arrogance is also part of the problem."

Jonathan raised his hands. "Enough. This isn't helping. We're supposed to be working together."

But the damage was done. The atmosphere in the room was tense, the team's unity splintering under the weight of their differences.

Sarah's Observation

After the meeting, Sarah pulled Jonathan aside. "We're struggling, Jonathan. Everyone's pointing fingers, but no one's looking at themselves."

Jonathan sighed, running a hand through his hair. "I know. It's ironic, isn't it? We're trying to restore love to the church, but we can't even show love to each other."

Sarah placed a hand on his arm. "This is part of the battle. Love isn't easy, especially when pride and fear get in the way. We need to confront this head-on, or we'll fail."

Jonathan nodded. "You're right. We'll start with me. If I'm not leading with love, how can I expect the team to follow?"

The Breaking Point

The tension reached a boiling point during a visit to a struggling church. The pastor had invited the team to share insights on reigniting discipleship, but the meeting quickly unraveled.

Reverend Harris, frustrated by the lack of progress, muttered, "This whole mission feels hopeless. We're trying to fix a broken system with a broken team."

Kayla, visibly hurt, shot back, "So what, we just give up? Maybe the real problem is that you've already written us off."

Elder Samuel, who rarely spoke out, surprised everyone by slamming his notebook shut. "Enough! We're all acting like spoiled children. Do you think the church's problems are worse than our own pride and stubbornness? We're no better than the people we're trying to help."

The room fell silent, his words striking a nerve.

Self-Reflection

That evening, the team gathered back at Jonathan's home, subdued and quiet. No one wanted to speak, but the unspoken tension hung heavy in the air. Finally, Sarah broke the silence.

"We need to talk about what's really going on here," she said gently. "We're fighting with each other because we're afraid. Afraid of failing, afraid of being wrong, afraid of being vulnerable. But love casts out fear, doesn't it?"

Kayla nodded slowly. "I've been so focused on proving myself that I forgot why I'm here in the first place."

Pastor Clark rubbed his temples. "And I've been trying to control everything because I hate feeling out of control. I thought I was defending the truth, but maybe I was just defending my pride."

Father Martinez spoke softly. "We're mirrors of the very problem we're trying to fix. If we can't love one another, how can we expect the church to change?"

Healing Through Honesty

Jonathan stood, his voice steady but filled with emotion. "We've been avoiding the truth, and the truth is this: we're all broken. We've let our differences divide us instead of letting love unite us. If we're going to restore love to the church, it has to start with us."

One by one, the team members confessed their struggles, their pride, and their fears. It was raw and uncomfortable, but as they spoke, the barriers between them began to crumble.

Deaconess Ruth reached for Pastor Clark's hand. "I'm sorry for dismissing your perspective. You're right—the Word is critical. I just want to make sure it's lived out."

Pastor Clark squeezed her hand, a rare smile breaking through. "And I'm sorry for being so rigid. You're right—we need to show love, not just talk about it."

Reverend Harris, Kayla, and Elder Samuel followed suit, each expressing their own apologies and commitments to moving forward in love.

A Renewed Commitment

As the evening wound down, the team knelt together in prayer. This time, their words weren't just petitions for the church—they were cries for personal transformation.

"Lord," Jonathan prayed, "break us down where we need to be broken. Heal us where we need healing. And fill us with Your love, so we can share it with others. Help us to be the example we want the church to follow."

When they rose from their knees, the atmosphere in the room was different. The tension was gone, replaced by a quiet sense of unity. They were still a diverse group with different perspectives, but now they were united by something greater: humility, forgiveness, and a shared desire to reflect Christ's love.

The battle within wasn't over, but they had taken a critical step forward. If they could love one another despite their differences, they could show the church—and the world—that love truly was the foundation of everything.

Part 3: The Spiritual War

Chapter 15: The Enemy's Agenda

The night was unusually still, the kind of quiet that seemed to hum with tension. Pastor Jonathan had called the team together for prayer after their recent breakthrough. They were finally finding unity, but something felt off—as if an unseen force was working to undermine their progress. That night, they would learn that their battle was far greater than they imagined.

A Vision Unfolds

As they prayed, Kayla suddenly froze. Her hands trembled, and she gripped the edge of the table. Her breathing quickened as she whispered, "I see something... it's dark... so dark."

The team exchanged uneasy glances, but Father Martinez stepped closer, his voice calm. "What do you see, Kayla? Speak it out."

Kayla closed her eyes, her voice trembling. "It's... a gathering. They're not human—shadowy, twisted figures. They're... mocking us. Laughing at the church."

Pastor Clark leaned forward, his expression intense. "What are they doing?"

"They're planning," Kayla said. "It's like a war room, but... perverse. Maps spread out before them, marked with the names of churches. Strings crisscross the maps, connecting people, congregations, and entire denominations. They're... targeting us."

The War Room of Darkness

Kayla's description painted a vivid picture of the demonic realm. In her vision, she saw a massive, cavernous space lit by an unnatural, flickering glow. Shadowy figures—demons—moved about with purpose, their faces grotesque and their eyes glowing with malice.

At the center of the room sat a figure larger than the rest, its presence commanding and terrifying. Its voice was a low growl, yet its words carried a chilling clarity. "Divide them. Distract them. Drain their love, and they will destroy themselves."

The demons cackled as they plotted, delighting in the chaos they were unleashing. Their strategies were sinister and methodical:

- **Division:** "Let their differences consume them. Turn doctrine into a weapon. Make unity seem impossible."
- **Distraction:** "Fill their lives with noise and busyness. Keep them so focused on their programs and numbers that they forget their purpose."
- **Deception:** "Convince them they are righteous while their hearts grow cold. Blind them to their own pride and selfishness."

Kayla's voice broke. "They're laughing at us. They think we're easy prey."

The Reality of Spiritual Warfare

When Kayla finished speaking, the room was silent, the weight of her vision settling over the team. Jonathan's heart pounded as he flipped open his Bible to Ephesians 6:12 and read aloud: *"For we wrestle not against flesh and blood, but against principalities, against powers, against the rulers of the darkness of this world, against spiritual wickedness in high places."*

"This is what we're up against," he said, his voice steady but filled with urgency. "The chaos in the church, the division, the apathy—it's not just human nature. It's the enemy's plan."

Deaconess Ruth stood, her expression fierce. "And we've been falling right into their trap. Every time we argue, every time we let fear or pride take over, we're doing their work for them."

Father Martinez added, "But we're not powerless. The enemy's agenda may be clear, but so is ours. Love is our weapon, and unity is our shield. They cannot stand against the Spirit of God."

A Glimpse of Hope

As the team prayed, another vision came to Kayla. This time, it was of light piercing the darkness. Flames began to appear on the maps she had seen before, one by one, growing brighter and spreading until the entire map was ablaze.

"They're afraid of us," she whispered, her voice stronger now. "They're afraid of what will happen if the church wakes up. If we remember our love, their plans will fail."

Pastor Clark stood, his usual stern demeanor softened by conviction. "We've been playing defense for too long. It's time to go on the offensive."

Jonathan nodded. "But not with weapons of this world. This battle is spiritual, and we fight it with prayer, Scripture, and love."

The Enemy's Fear

The team spent the rest of the night in prayer, interceding for the church and standing against the schemes of the enemy. As they prayed, they felt a renewed sense of purpose—a holy determination to push back the darkness.

Reverend Harris spoke softly, quoting 2 Corinthians 10:4: *"The weapons we fight with are not the weapons of the world. On the contrary, they have divine power to demolish strongholds."*

"We need to remember this," he said. "The enemy's agenda is powerful, but it's not unstoppable. If we stand together, rooted in Christ, they don't stand a chance."

A New Perspective

As dawn broke, the team left Jonathan's home, their hearts heavy but hopeful. They now understood the true scope of their mission. It wasn't just about restoring love to the church—it was about reclaiming territory from the enemy.

Sarah walked beside Jonathan, her voice quiet. "Do you think we're ready for this?"

Jonathan looked up at the sky, the first rays of sunlight breaking through the darkness. "We have to be. The church is God's plan for the world, and He's given us everything we need to win this fight. We just have to trust Him."

The battle lines had been drawn, and the enemy's agenda was clear. But so was the team's resolve. They were no longer just investigators—they were warriors in a spiritual war, armed with faith, prayer, and the unshakable love of Christ.

Chapter 16: The Power of Unity

The team gathered at a retreat center on the outskirts of the city, surrounded by a dense forest that seemed to embrace them in its quiet stillness. It had been days since Kayla's vision of the demonic realm and the enemy's agenda, and the weight of their mission hung heavily on their hearts. Tonight, they were seeking clarity—not just for their next steps, but for the deeper question of how to restore love to the church.

As they settled into a circle of chairs, Sarah stood to address the group. "We've seen the problem clearly—division, pride, fear. But the real question is, how do we move forward? How do we restore love when it feels like everything is working against us?"

Jonathan opened his Bible, his voice steady but solemn. "I believe the answer lies in unity. Not just a superficial agreement, but true unity in Christ. That's the only way we can overcome the enemy's agenda and fulfill our mission."

The Call to Unity

Father Martinez nodded, turning to John 17:21. "Jesus prayed for this very thing. *'I pray that they will all be one, just as You and I are one—as You are in Me, Father, and I am in You. And may they be in us so that the world will believe You sent Me.'*"

Kayla leaned forward, her voice thoughtful. "Unity isn't just a nice idea—it's essential. Jesus said the world would know Him through our unity. If we're divided, how can we expect the world to see Christ in us?"

Deaconess Ruth added, "But unity isn't the same as uniformity. We don't have to agree on every detail, but we do need to be united in our purpose—to love God, love others, and make disciples."

Reverend Harris adjusted his glasses. "Unity without repentance is meaningless. If we're going to come together, we need to acknowledge our failings—both as individuals and as the church—and seek forgiveness."

Repentance in Action

Jonathan led the team in a time of self-reflection. "Let's start by confessing where we've fallen short. We can't call the church to repentance if we're not willing to repent ourselves."

Pastor Clark was the first to speak, his voice heavy with emotion. "I've been so focused on being right that I've forgotten how to love. I've judged others harshly, including all of you. I'm sorry."

Kayla wiped a tear from her cheek. "I've held back out of fear—fear of being rejected, fear of failure. I've let that fear stop me from loving people the way God calls me to."

Father Martinez spoke next, his tone calm but sincere. "I've allowed my pride to create walls between myself and others. I've looked down on those who don't share my traditions, and for that, I ask forgiveness."

One by one, the team confessed their struggles, their pride, and their failures. As they spoke, the atmosphere in the room began to change. The walls of tension and distrust that had lingered for weeks crumbled, replaced by an overwhelming sense of humility and grace.

The Power of the Cross

Sarah stood, her eyes filled with tears. "This is what unity looks like—not perfection, but humility and forgiveness. If we can do this, the church can, too. But it starts with repentance."

Jonathan turned to Ephesians 4:2-3 and read aloud:
'Be completely humble and gentle; be patient, bearing with one another in love. Make every effort to keep the unity of the Spirit through the bond of peace.'

"We can't create unity on our own," he said. "It's the Spirit who unites us, and that unity is built on the foundation of Christ's love."

A Moment of Breakthrough

As the team prayed together, a profound sense of peace filled the room. It wasn't just the absence of conflict—it was the presence of something holy, something greater than themselves.

Kayla spoke softly, her eyes closed. "I see the flame again... but this time, it's in us. It's small, but it's growing. It's connecting us, like threads of light weaving us together."

Deaconess Ruth smiled. "That's the Spirit at work. When we're united in Christ, the flame of His love burns brighter."

Jonathan stood, his voice steady with conviction. "This is the key. Unity in Christ, rooted in repentance and love. If we want to restore love to the church, we have to show them what it looks like. And it starts with us."

Moving Forward

The team left the retreat center with a renewed sense of purpose. They had learned that unity wasn't about agreement—it was about surrender. Surrendering their pride, their fears, and their agendas to Christ, and allowing His Spirit to bind them together.

As they walked back to their cars, Pastor Clark turned to Jonathan. "Do you really think the church can change? That we can overcome all this division?"

Jonathan looked up at the night sky, the stars shining brightly. "I believe it's possible. But it starts with us. If we can live out the unity and love we've been called to, others will follow. And when the church is united, nothing can stop it—not even the gates of hell."

The team drove away that night, knowing they had crossed a critical threshold. They weren't just a group of individuals anymore—they were one body, united in Christ, and ready to take the next steps in their mission to restore love to the church.

Chapter 17: A Vision of the Bride

The team gathered in the sanctuary of a small, rustic chapel for their weekly prayer meeting. The simplicity of the space, with its wooden pews and a single cross hanging above the altar, provided a perfect backdrop for their ongoing quest to restore love to the church. Tonight, they felt an urgency in their prayers, as if something significant was about to be revealed.

Kayla, still shaken by the visions she had experienced before, sat quietly near the front, her Bible open but untouched. She had been praying for clarity, asking God to show her more of what was happening in the spiritual realm. As the team began to pray, she felt a familiar warmth settle over her—a presence she had come to recognize as the Holy Spirit.

The Vision Begins

Suddenly, Kayla gasped, her hands clutching the edge of the pew. Her breathing quickened, and her eyes closed tightly. The others immediately gathered around her, their concern evident.

"Kayla, what is it?" Sarah asked gently, placing a hand on her shoulder.

Kayla's voice trembled. "I... I see her. The Bride. But she's... she's not as she should be."

Her words sent a chill through the group. Jonathan knelt beside her. "What do you see? Tell us."

The Stained Bride

In her vision, Kayla saw a radiant figure—a bride standing at the edge of a great banquet hall. She was clothed in a wedding gown that once must have been breathtaking, but now it was torn and stained. The fabric was marred by mud, ash, and crimson streaks, as if she had been walking through a battlefield.

The bride held a bouquet of wilted flowers, her hands trembling as she approached a great throne at the end of the hall. Her head was bowed, not in reverence, but in shame. Around her, shadowy figures whispered accusations, their voices dripping with malice.

"She's unworthy."
"She's forgotten her love."
"She's consumed by herself."

Kayla's voice broke. "She's... stained with pride and selfishness. Her gown is torn by division and her hands are heavy with guilt. She knows she's supposed to be beautiful, but she's ashamed of what she's become."

The Voice of the Groom

But then, Kayla's tone shifted, her trembling voice steadied by a sudden presence in the vision. "I see Him," she whispered, tears streaming down her face. "The Groom is coming."

The team held their breath as Kayla described the scene. The Bride lifted her head, her eyes wide with fear and longing. The shadowy figures scattered as a brilliant light filled the room. The Groom stepped forward, His presence commanding and filled with love.

He spoke softly but firmly. *"You are My Bride. You are called to be pure and holy, without spot or wrinkle. But you have forgotten your first love. Return to Me, and I will restore you. Repent, and I will make you new."*

As He spoke, the stains on the Bride's gown began to fade. The tears in the fabric mended, and her bouquet bloomed again. She stood taller, her shame replaced by a radiant joy as she moved toward her Groom.

The Team's Response

When the vision ended, Kayla opened her eyes, her cheeks wet with tears. "He's calling us to return to Him," she said, her voice shaking. "The Bride—the church—has forgotten her first love. We've been consumed by pride, selfishness, and division. But He hasn't given up on us. He's waiting for us to repent so He can restore us."

The room was silent, the weight of the vision sinking into their hearts. Jonathan stood, his voice heavy with emotion. "This is the heart of our mission. The church isn't beyond saving, but we need to lead her back to her Groom. It starts with repentance, humility, and love."

Father Martinez added, "This vision isn't just a warning—it's an invitation. Christ is calling His church to return to Him, to prepare herself for His coming. We've been distracted, but He's reminding us of who we are: His Bride."

A Renewed Commitment

The team knelt together in prayer, their hearts heavy but hopeful. One by one, they prayed for the church—for repentance, healing, and restoration. They prayed for unity among believers and for the courage to live out the love they had been called to share.

As they rose, Sarah spoke softly. "The stains can be washed away. The division can be healed. But we have to be willing to fight for the Bride—not with weapons, but with love."

Jonathan nodded. "And we have to start now. The Groom is coming, and the church must be ready."

The Call to Action

The vision of the stained Bride was a turning point for the team. It gave them a clear picture of the church's current state and a powerful reminder of Christ's love and faithfulness. They left the chapel that night with renewed determination, knowing their mission wasn't just about restoring love—it was about preparing the Bride of Christ for her Groom.

The stakes had never been higher, but neither had their hope. The Bride wasn't perfect, but she was loved, and her Groom was waiting with open arms. It was time to help her find her way back.

Chapter 18: The World Speaks

The team decided to venture beyond the walls of the church, seeking to understand how the outside world perceived Christianity. They believed that listening to non-believers might offer valuable insight into the church's failures—and perhaps a clue to restoring its role as a beacon of love and hope.

Jonathan arranged a series of informal focus groups in a local community center. Flyers advertised an open invitation to anyone willing to share their honest opinions about the church. The response was greater than expected. Over the course of a week, the team spoke with dozens of people—students, professionals, skeptics, and even those who had once been part of the church but had left.

What they heard would shake them to their core.

The Stories of Disappointment

On the first night, the room was filled with a mix of curiosity and tension. A young woman named Jasmine, who had grown up in the church but left in her twenties, was the first to speak. Her words were direct and unapologetic.

"I left because I didn't feel loved," she said, her arms crossed. "I was judged for everything—what I wore, the questions I asked, even the friends I had. It felt like the church cared more about appearances than people."

A man in his thirties named Carlos nodded. "Same here. When my wife and I went through a rough patch, we reached out for help, but all we got was advice that felt like a script. No one actually listened to us. We felt like we didn't matter."

Others chimed in:

- "It feels like the church is more interested in condemning people than helping them."
- "I grew up hearing about God's love, but I never saw it in action."
- "The church just seems fake to me. It's like they're playing a role instead of being real."

The team listened in silence, each comment cutting deeper than the last. Kayla scribbled notes furiously, her hand trembling. "We've lost our witness," she whispered to Jonathan.

Confronting Hypocrisy

One man, an outspoken atheist named Mark, leaned forward in his chair, his tone sharp but not hostile. "You want to know why people don't trust the church? It's because you don't practice what you preach. You talk about love and forgiveness, but you're some of the most judgmental people out there. You're quick to point out the world's sins but blind to your own."

Pastor Clark, uncharacteristically quiet, finally spoke. "What would it take for you to trust the church again?"

Mark shrugged. "Honesty. Humility. Stop pretending you're better than everyone else. Admit that you're flawed, just like the rest of us. And actually love people—not because you're trying to 'save' them, but because you care."

His words hung in the air, heavy with truth.

Hope Among the Criticism

Not all the feedback was negative. A few attendees shared stories of times when the church had made a difference in their lives.

"I remember one pastor who visited me in the hospital every day when I was sick," an elderly woman named Margaret shared. "He didn't try to preach at me—he just sat with me and prayed. That meant more to me than any sermon."

A college student named Leah added, "I had a youth leader who really cared about us. She didn't judge me for my mistakes—she helped me through them. That's the kind of love I wish I saw more of."

These stories reminded the team that the church's potential to love and serve was still alive, even if it had been overshadowed by its failures.

The Team's Reflection

That evening, the team gathered to process what they had heard. The weight of the criticism had left them shaken but determined.

Sarah broke the silence. "We've been so focused on what the church is doing internally, but we've forgotten how the world sees us. If we're going to restore love, we need to start by rebuilding trust."

Reverend Harris nodded solemnly. "It's humbling, isn't it? We preach about humility and grace, but we've failed to live it out. The world isn't asking for perfection—they're asking for sincerity."

Pastor Clark, his voice uncharacteristically soft, added, "Mark's words keep ringing in my ears. We need to stop acting like we have it all together. The truth is, we don't. But maybe if we admit that, we can start to heal."

Jonathan leaned forward, his voice filled with conviction. "The world is speaking, and we can't ignore them. Their disappointment isn't just criticism—it's a cry for help. They want to see the love of Christ, not just hear about it. And it's our job to show it."

A Call to Action

The team decided to act immediately. They outlined three key steps:

1. **Listening:** Continue creating spaces for non-believers to share their experiences and perspectives.
2. **Serving:** Organize tangible acts of love and service in the community without any agenda or strings attached.
3. **Humility:** Be honest about the church's flaws and lead with repentance and vulnerability.

As they prayed together, they felt a renewed sense of purpose. The feedback from the world wasn't just criticism—it was a wake-up call. The church had been blind to its own failings, but now they saw clearly. And they were ready to change.

Jonathan closed the meeting with a prayer. "Lord, thank You for opening our eyes. Forgive us for where we've fallen short, and help us to be the light You've called us to be. Teach us to love as You love, so that the world may see You in us. Amen."

The team left the community center that night with heavy hearts but hopeful spirits. The world had spoken, and now it was their turn to respond—with action, humility, and the unwavering love of Christ.

Chapter 19: The Cost of Love

It began with an unexpected email. Pastor Jonathan read the message in silence, his face tightening as he scrolled through the words. The sender was an influential figure in the local community, a businessman named Greg Stanton, whose name carried weight in both political and religious circles. Stanton had long been critical of Jonathan's efforts to unite churches across denominations, often dismissing it as "a waste of time."

The email was a simple invitation: a public forum to debate the relevance of the modern church. The timing couldn't have been worse, but the team agreed that this was an opportunity to demonstrate love, even in the face of opposition.

The forum quickly devolved into an ambush. Stanton's questions were pointed, his tone sharp as he criticized the church for its failures. He accused Jonathan and his team of compromising doctrine, catering to the world, and neglecting the "true gospel." The audience, filled with Stanton's supporters, erupted into applause at every jab.

Jonathan remained calm, but it was Kayla who finally stood. What happened next would change everything.

Kayla's Decision

Kayla rose from her seat, her heart pounding. Stanton turned to her, a thin smile on his face. "Ah, one of Pastor Jonathan's team members. Please, enlighten us."

She hesitated, glancing at Jonathan, who gave her a slight nod. Taking a deep breath, she stepped forward to the microphone. "Mr. Stanton, I hear your frustrations. The church has failed in many ways, and we've fallen short of what Christ has called us to be. But I believe love—not condemnation—is the way forward."

The room fell silent. Stanton raised an eyebrow. "Love? Tell me, how far are you willing to go for this so-called love? Would you defend the church's failures, its compromises? Would you stand by those who twist Scripture to suit their agendas?"

Kayla's voice wavered, but she didn't back down. "Love doesn't mean ignoring sin or truth. It means showing grace even when it's undeserved. It means standing with those who are broken, even when it costs us something."

Stanton's smile faded. "So, you're saying the church should abandon its principles to embrace the world?"

"No," Kayla said firmly. "I'm saying the church should embrace the world with the same love Christ showed—sacrificial, radical, and unconditional."

The Accusation

As Kayla finished speaking, Stanton leaned into the microphone, his tone cutting. "You speak of love, but what about the people who reject God's truth? What about those who mock the church, who live in open rebellion? Would you stand with them, too?"

Kayla paused, the weight of his question sinking in. She thought of Jasmine, the young woman from the focus group who had left the church after feeling judged. She thought of Mark, the outspoken atheist who demanded honesty from Christians. And she thought of Jesus, who ate with tax collectors and sinners, who loved even as He was nailed to the cross.

"Yes," she said finally, her voice steady. "I would."

The room erupted. Stanton's supporters jeered, some shaking their heads in disgust. "Compromiser!" someone shouted. "Traitor to the faith!" another called out.

Jonathan rose to intervene, but Kayla motioned for him to stay seated. She stepped closer to the microphone, her eyes scanning the crowd. "You can call me whatever you want. But if standing with the broken, the outcasts, and even my enemies makes me a compromiser, then so be it. That's what Jesus did, and I'll follow Him."

The Fallout

The forum ended in chaos. Stanton stormed out, declaring that Kayla's words were proof of the church's decline. Social media lit up with posts condemning her, labeling her as a false teacher, a liberal activist, and worse. Some members of the team's own congregations distanced themselves, calling for her removal from the group.

Kayla sat alone in the church that night, her heart heavy. She knew her words had been true, but the cost felt overwhelming. Her reputation, carefully built through years of faithful service, had been shattered in a single moment.

Sarah found her sitting in the front pew. "You did the right thing," she said softly, sitting beside her.

Kayla shook her head. "Did I? The whole city thinks I've betrayed the church. Maybe I went too far."

Sarah placed a hand on her shoulder. "Jesus went farther. He was mocked, ridiculed, and rejected for loving the unlovable. You followed His example, and that's what matters."

The Team's Support

The next morning, the team gathered to discuss the fallout. Pastor Clark, who had been one of the harshest critics of compromise, was the first to speak.

"I'll admit," he began, "when you spoke last night, I cringed. I thought you were playing into Stanton's hands. But then I realized... you were right. Love costs something. And if we're not willing to pay the price, what kind of witnesses are we?"

Father Martinez nodded. "Kayla showed us what radical love looks like. It's not easy, and it's not always understood, but it's what Christ calls us to."

Jonathan smiled. "This is the kind of love that changes hearts—not just in the church, but in the world. Kayla, you showed them what it means to follow Jesus, even when it hurts."

A Ripple Effect

Despite the criticism, Kayla's words began to resonate. A week later, Jasmine reached out to her, thanking her for her courage. "I've never heard anyone talk about love like that," she said. "It made me want to give the church another chance."

Others followed, sharing stories of how her stand had reminded them of the love they had once experienced in the church but thought was gone. Slowly, the tide began to turn.

Kayla's sacrifice had come at a cost, but it bore fruit. It reminded the team—and the church—that love isn't about preserving reputations or winning arguments. It's about showing Christ's heart, no matter the price.

Chapter 20: The Underground Church

The team had been invited by a pastor in a neighboring city to visit a group of believers who, unlike the larger congregations they had encountered, operated quietly and intentionally under the radar. Known only as "The Fellowship," this small community met in homes, backyards, and sometimes even in hidden basements. They weren't underground in the literal sense of persecution, but their approach to faith was countercultural and deeply rooted in love and discipleship.

Jonathan was intrigued. "If there's a group living out what we're striving for, we need to learn from them."

The Hidden Gathering

The team arrived at an unassuming house on the outskirts of town. There was no sign, no parking lot, no indication that anything unusual was happening. Inside, they were greeted warmly by a middle-aged woman named Clara, one of the group's leaders. Her smile was genuine, and her eyes sparkled with a quiet confidence.

"Welcome," she said, ushering them into the living room, where about twenty people of various ages sat in a circle. Some held Bibles; others simply listened as a young man shared a testimony about how the group's love and support had helped him recover from addiction.

Jonathan and the team watched in awe. There were no microphones, no polished presentations, just raw, authentic faith. As the young man finished, the group gathered around him, laying hands on him and praying. Their prayers were heartfelt, each word filled with compassion.

Living Out Love

After the gathering, Clara invited the team to stay for a meal.
As they sat at a long table laden with simple but delicious food,
Clara began to share the group's story.

"We're not against the institutional church," she explained. "But
we felt like it was losing something—something vital. So, we
decided to strip everything back and focus on the essentials:
loving God, loving others, and making disciples."

Father Martinez nodded. "You've certainly succeeded. There's
a depth here that's rare to see."

Clara smiled. "It hasn't been easy. We're not perfect, but we
hold each other accountable. We don't just meet on Sundays;
we live life together. When someone struggles, we show up.
When someone rejoices, we celebrate. It's messy, but it's real."

Stories of Sacrifice

The team spent the evening hearing stories from the members.
A single mother shared how the group had stepped in to
babysit her children and provide meals when she lost her job. A
retired teacher recounted how he had been discipled by a
younger member, learning to embrace a new season of
ministry.

One man, an immigrant named Adeel, told his story through a
translator. He had fled his home country due to religious
persecution and found refuge in The Fellowship.

"When I came here," he said, his voice thick with emotion, "I
was broken. I had lost everything—my home, my family, my

church. But these people... they became my family. They didn't just preach to me; they loved me."

Kayla wiped a tear from her cheek. "This is what the church is supposed to look like."

The Secret of Discipleship

Before the team left, Clara shared the principles that guided their group.

"We keep it simple," she said. "First, we focus on relationships. Discipleship isn't a program; it's walking alongside people in their everyday lives. Second, we prioritize prayer and the Word. That's our foundation. And third, we practice sacrificial love. That means putting others first, even when it's inconvenient."

Jonathan nodded. "You've rediscovered the heart of the church. What you're doing here is exactly what we've been searching for."

Clara's expression turned serious. "It's not a secret formula. It's the way Jesus lived. But it requires surrender. You have to let go of your pride, your preferences, and your comfort."

A Call to Action

As the team drove home that night, the atmosphere in the car was quiet, each of them lost in thought. Finally, Pastor Clark spoke. "I thought I understood discipleship, but tonight... I realized how shallow my efforts have been."

Reverend Harris added, "It's humbling, isn't it? They don't have the resources or the platforms that we do, but they've done more to reflect Christ than most of our churches combined."

Jonathan gripped the steering wheel. "It's not about resources. It's about love. They've shown us what's possible when love and discipleship are at the center."

Sarah turned to the group. "We can't just admire what they're doing. We need to act. What if we started modeling this kind of love in our own churches? What if we trained others to do the same?"

Learning from the Underground

The team spent the next week debriefing, reflecting on what they had learned from The Fellowship. They began to implement small changes in their own communities, emphasizing relationships over programs and putting a renewed focus on prayer and discipleship.

Their visit to the underground church had opened their eyes to what was possible. It reminded them that the church wasn't about buildings, events, or systems—it was about people living out the radical, sacrificial love of Christ.

And for the first time in their journey, they felt that the flame of love was beginning to grow.

Chapter 21: The Spiritual Weapons

The team reconvened after their transformative visit to the underground church, filled with inspiration but also a sense of urgency. They now understood that restoring love to the church would require more than human effort. It was a spiritual battle, and they needed spiritual weapons to fight it.

The Call to Spiritual Warfare

Pastor Jonathan opened the meeting with a somber tone. "We've seen the enemy's agenda. We've heard the world's disappointment. We've even glimpsed what the church is supposed to be. But none of it will matter if we don't fight this battle the right way."

Father Martinez nodded, turning to Ephesians 6:10-18. "Paul told us to put on the full armor of God. This isn't a metaphor—it's a command. Prayer, fasting, and the Word of God aren't just disciplines; they're our weapons."

Deaconess Ruth stood, her voice resolute. "Then it's time we stopped talking about love and started fighting for it. But first, we need to make sure our own hearts are right."

Weapon 1: Prayer

The team decided to dedicate the next several days to focused prayer, each member taking shifts to ensure someone was always interceding. They met at dawn for corporate prayer, crying out for God to restore love in the church and to purify their own hearts.

Kayla, who had struggled with fear throughout their journey, felt a breakthrough during one of these sessions. "Lord," she prayed aloud, "help me to love boldly, even when it's hard. Teach me to see people the way You do."

As they prayed, the atmosphere in the room began to shift. Tensions eased, and their unity grew stronger. They began to feel the weight of God's presence, as if He was affirming their efforts.

Weapon 2: Fasting

Sarah suggested adding fasting to their spiritual arsenal. "Jesus said some things only come out through prayer and fasting. If we're serious about this mission, we need to be willing to sacrifice."

Each team member chose a specific fast—some abstained from food, others from distractions like social media or entertainment. The fasting wasn't easy, but it brought clarity and focus.

Pastor Clark, who had struggled with pride, shared a moment of vulnerability during their evening meeting. "Fasting has shown me how much I rely on myself instead of God. I've been asking Him to change the church, but I'm realizing He needs to change me first."

Weapon 3: The Word

Elder Samuel suggested a deeper dive into Scripture, focusing on passages about love, unity, and spiritual warfare. They divided the work, each member studying different sections and sharing their insights.

Jonathan led a session on 1 Corinthians 13. "This chapter is often read at weddings, but it's a battle plan for the church. Without love, nothing we do matters—our gifts, our actions, even our faith. Love is the weapon that disarms the enemy."

Reverend Harris delved into John 15, emphasizing the importance of abiding in Christ. "If we're not connected to the vine, we can't bear fruit. Restoring love starts with being rooted in Him."

Kayla brought insights from 2 Corinthians 10:4-5:
'The weapons we fight with are not the weapons of the world. On the contrary, they have divine power to demolish strongholds.'
She added, "We've been trying to fix this with programs and strategies, but the real fight is in the spiritual realm."

A Renewed Heart

As the days passed, the team began to notice changes in themselves. Old frustrations and divisions faded as they humbled themselves before God. Their prayers grew bolder, their unity stronger, and their love for one another deeper.

Sarah reflected during one of their meetings. "This is what's been missing—not just in the church, but in us. Prayer, fasting, and the Word aren't just tools; they're the way we stay connected to God's heart. And His heart is love."

A Test of Faith

Their new resolve was tested when they received news of another challenge. A prominent local leader had publicly criticized their mission, calling it "idealistic" and "out of touch with reality." The team felt the sting of the attack, but instead of reacting in anger, they chose to pray for the critic.

"We're not fighting against flesh and blood," Jonathan reminded them. "This is exactly why we need to stay focused on the spiritual battle."

Victory in the Spirit

One night, as they gathered for prayer, Kayla had another vision. She saw the church as a vast battlefield, with believers standing side by side, their hands clasped in prayer. As they prayed, chains began to fall from those around them, and a brilliant light spread across the battlefield.

"The battle isn't won by fighting each other," she said, her voice trembling. "It's won by standing together, rooted in Christ and armed with His love."

Her vision reignited their passion. They realized that the restoration of love in the church wasn't just about programs or teachings—it was about a spiritual renewal that started in their own hearts and spread outward.

Moving Forward

With their spiritual weapons sharpened, the team felt ready to take the next steps in their mission. They knew the road ahead would be difficult, but they also knew they weren't fighting alone.

As Jonathan closed their final meeting of the week, he prayed, "Lord, thank You for teaching us to fight Your way. Help us to carry these lessons forward, not just for ourselves, but for the church and the world. Let Your love flow through us, breaking chains and bringing light to the darkness. Amen."

The team left that night, united and emboldened. They were no longer just a group of believers—they were warriors, armed with prayer, fasting, and the Word, ready to restore love to the church and fulfill their mission.

Part 4: Restoring Love

Chapter 22: The First Church Transformed

The team's journey had led them back to Pastor Jonathan's home church, Grace Community Church. It was here, weeks ago, that the team had witnessed division and judgment rear their ugly heads, especially toward the worldly visitors who had walked through their doors. Now, with a renewed understanding of love and a clear vision of their mission, the team felt compelled to help Grace Community lead the way.

A Call to Action

Jonathan stood before his congregation on a crisp Sunday morning, his heart pounding as he stepped up to the pulpit. The sanctuary was quieter than usual, the crowd noticeably smaller after weeks of controversy surrounding the team's mission.

Jonathan gripped the edges of the pulpit and began. "Brothers and sisters, we've been called to be the light of the world. But how can we be light if we refuse to love? How can we reflect Christ if we judge others for their brokenness while ignoring our own?"

He paused, his voice steady but emotional. "We've failed to love. I've failed to love. And it's time to change."

Jonathan then shared the stories of the visitors who had felt unwelcome—the young man with brightly dyed hair, the single mother struggling to find hope, and others who had come seeking refuge but had been met with judgment instead of grace.

"Starting today," he said firmly, "this church will be a house of love. We will embrace everyone who walks through these doors, no matter where they've come from or what they've done. And it will start with us."

A Challenge to Change

After the sermon, Jonathan invited the congregation to join him in prayer. "If we're going to change, it has to begin with repentance," he said. "We can't expect the world to see Christ in us if we're unwilling to admit where we've gone wrong."

As he knelt at the altar, something unexpected happened. One by one, members of the congregation began to join him. Some wept openly, confessing their pride and prejudice. Others prayed silently, their faces etched with conviction.

Welcoming the Outcasts

The following week, Jonathan and Sarah reached out to the visitors who had felt rejected, inviting them to return. To their surprise, many agreed, albeit hesitantly.

The young man with the brightly dyed hair, whose name was Sam, was the first to arrive. He lingered in the back of the sanctuary, clearly uncertain. A few church members glanced his way, but this time, there were no judgmental stares or whispered comments. Instead, Deaconess Ruth walked over and greeted him warmly.

"Sam, it's good to see you," she said with a smile. "You're welcome here."

Sam nodded slowly, still unsure, but he stayed. As the service progressed, other visitors arrived—the single mother with her two children, an older man who appeared homeless, and even a few teens who had been labeled as troublemakers.

A Visible Transformation

The turning point came during the altar call. Jonathan invited anyone who needed prayer to come forward, and to his surprise, Sam was the first to step forward. Tears streamed down his face as he confessed his struggles and doubts, his voice trembling.

The congregation watched in silence, unsure of how to respond. Then, an elderly woman named Mrs. Elkins, who had previously been one of the most vocal critics of the team's mission, stepped forward. She placed a hand on Sam's shoulder and began to pray, her voice filled with compassion.

It was a moment that shifted the atmosphere. Other members began to follow her example, surrounding Sam and the other visitors with love and prayer. For the first time in years, Grace Community felt like a true reflection of Christ's body.

Stories of Change

Over the next few weeks, the church continued to embrace the call to love. Sam became a regular attendee, even volunteering to help with the church's outreach programs. The single mother found a supportive community that helped her find a job and care for her children. The older man who appeared homeless revealed he had been a former pastor who had fallen on hard times; the church rallied around him, helping him find housing and rediscovering his faith.

Jonathan watched with amazement as the church transformed before his eyes. The once-judgmental congregation had become a beacon of hope and love, reaching out to those they had once rejected.

The Ripple Effect

Word of Grace Community's transformation began to spread. Other pastors and church leaders in the area took notice, reaching out to Jonathan and his team for guidance. The team shared what they had learned: that love wasn't just a feeling but an action rooted in humility, repentance, and the Spirit's power.

Kayla summed it up during one of their meetings. "When we welcomed those visitors back, we weren't just inviting them into a church service. We were showing them the heart of God. And that's what people are longing for."

A New Beginning

On a bright Sunday morning, Jonathan stood before his congregation once again, but this time, the sanctuary was full—not just with people, but with joy, hope, and love.

"This is just the beginning," he said, his voice filled with conviction. "We've seen what happens when we choose love. Now, it's time to take it beyond these walls. Let's be the church that Christ has called us to be."

The congregation erupted in applause, not out of formality but out of genuine excitement for the journey ahead. Grace Community had been transformed, and it was now a shining example of what the church could be when love was at the center.

The Team's Reflection

As the team gathered later that day, Sarah looked around the room and smiled. "This is what we've been working for. It's proof that love can change hearts—starting with us."

Jonathan nodded. "And if one church can be transformed, so can others. This is just the beginning."

The team left that night with renewed hope, knowing that the flame of love had been reignited—and it was only a matter of time before it spread.

Chapter 23: The Ripple Effect

News of Grace Community Church's transformation spread quickly. What started as a small, local effort to restore love had sparked something much larger—a movement that began to touch churches across denominations. Pastors and congregations, inspired by the stories of radical repentance, humility, and unity, began reaching out to Jonathan and his team for guidance.

The flame of love that had been reignited in one church was now spreading like wildfire.

A Network of Change

The team set up a series of workshops and meetings, inviting leaders from various denominations to learn about the principles that had transformed Grace Community. These gatherings were unlike anything the churches had experienced before. Instead of focusing on strategies or programs, the workshops emphasized prayer, repentance, and the power of unity in Christ.

Kayla led a session on humility. "We can't talk about love without first admitting where we've failed. Love requires vulnerability, and that starts with us as leaders."

Father Martinez shared about the importance of unity. "Christ prayed that His followers would be one, just as He and the Father are one. Unity doesn't mean uniformity—it means setting aside our differences to focus on what matters most: loving God and loving others."

Pastor Clark, who had once struggled with rigid pride, now passionately spoke about grace. "We've spent too much time building walls between denominations. It's time to break them down and let love flow freely."

Churches Transformed

Over the next few months, the ripple effect began to take hold. Congregations that had been marked by division, legalism, and complacency began to change. Stories of transformation poured in:

- **A Traditional Baptist Church:** A congregation that had once prided itself on strict adherence to doctrine began to embrace the broken and hurting in their community. Their Sunday services became known for heartfelt worship and testimonies of lives changed by love.
- **A Pentecostal Revival:** A church that had focused on fiery preaching and outward expressions of faith began to turn inward, focusing on discipleship and building authentic relationships among its members.
- **A Catholic Parish:** Inspired by Father Martinez, a parish began hosting ecumenical prayer nights, inviting members of other denominations to join them in seeking God's presence together.
- **A Non-Denominational Church:** Known for its flashy services, this church stripped back its programming to focus on small groups, where members learned to live out love in tangible ways.

The Revival Spreads

As the movement grew, it extended beyond church walls. Entire communities began to feel the impact of this revival of love:

- Homeless shelters were overwhelmed with volunteers from churches eager to serve.
- Broken families were reconciled through the prayers and efforts of church members.
- Local governments sought advice from church leaders on addressing societal issues, recognizing the unique role of love in bringing about change.

Even skeptics and non-believers began to take notice. One local journalist, who had initially written a critical article about Grace Community's efforts, published a follow-up piece titled, *"When Love Leads: How the Church is Changing the City."*

A Meeting of Denominations

The team organized a historic gathering of churches from across the city—Baptist, Pentecostal, Catholic, Methodist, and others. Held in a neutral venue, the event was focused on prayer, worship, and testimonies of what God was doing through the revival of love.

Kayla stood before the crowd, her voice trembling with emotion. "We've seen what happens when love is restored. Walls come down, hearts are healed, and the world takes notice. But this is just the beginning. If we stay united in Christ, there's no limit to what He can do through us."

The gathering ended with a powerful time of worship, as leaders and members from every denomination knelt together in prayer. It was a glimpse of the unity Jesus had prayed for—a unity that transcended differences and focused on the love that bound them together.

The Team's Reflection

That evening, the team gathered to reflect on what they had witnessed. Pastor Clark, who had been skeptical of their mission at the start, spoke first. "I never thought I'd see this in my lifetime—churches working together, loving each other, setting aside their differences. This is what the kingdom of God looks like."

Reverend Harris nodded. "It's humbling, isn't it? To see what happens when we step out of the way and let God lead."

Jonathan looked around the room, his heart full. "This revival didn't start with a program or a strategy. It started with repentance. With prayer. With love. And it's spreading because people are seeing what happens when we truly follow Jesus."

A Movement Rooted in Love

The ripple effect of love was undeniable. Churches that had once been stagnant were now thriving. Communities that had been divided were now coming together. And the team, once a small group of believers searching for answers, had become catalysts for a movement that was transforming lives and restoring hope.

But they knew their work wasn't done.

As they bowed their heads in prayer, Sarah whispered, "Lord, let this flame of love never fade. Keep it burning bright, so that the world may see You through us."

The ripple effect had begun, but it was only the start of what God was doing. The church was awakening, love was being restored, and the Bride of Christ was preparing for her Groom.

Chapter 24: The Ultimate Test

The revival of love had sparked a fire across denominations, transforming churches and communities. But with that transformation came resistance. The team's efforts, now highly visible, drew the attention of not only church leaders and believers but also the media and those in positions of power who felt threatened by the unity and influence of the movement.

It began subtly—a few critical articles, online debates questioning their intentions, and whispers about whether their message was "too radical." But soon, the attacks became more direct.

The Media Strikes

A major news outlet aired a segment on the revival, framing it as "a dangerous blurring of religious boundaries." The anchor's voice dripped with skepticism as they questioned whether the team's efforts to unite churches and embrace outcasts compromised traditional Christian values.

"They're abandoning doctrine for emotionalism," one commentator said. "This so-called 'love movement' is just another way to water down the truth."

Another guest accused the team of political motives. "This is nothing more than an attempt to control people under the guise of faith."

The backlash was swift. Social media exploded with accusations, conspiracy theories, and calls to shut down the team's efforts. Some labeled them heretics; others called them sellouts.

Kayla, scrolling through the comments one night, felt her heart sink. "They don't understand," she whispered. "We're not trying to compromise the truth—we're trying to live it."

Jonathan put a reassuring hand on her shoulder. "This was bound to happen. Jesus warned us this would come."

The Legal Battle

As the media attacks escalated, so did the legal challenges. A prominent activist group filed a lawsuit against Grace Community Church, accusing the church of discrimination based on its previous actions toward marginalized groups. Though the church had repented and transformed, the lawsuit dredged up old wounds, painting their repentance as insincere.

"This is an attack on our faith," Pastor Clark said during an emergency meeting. "They're trying to discredit everything we've done."

Deaconess Ruth, ever the pragmatist, added, "We can't let this stop us. We need to fight, not just in court but on our knees. This isn't just a legal battle—it's spiritual warfare."

Jonathan agreed. "We'll cooperate with the legal process, but our focus has to remain on love and truth. We can't let fear or anger dictate our response."

Standing Firm in Love

The team decided to respond with the same love they had been preaching. They released a public statement, acknowledging their past failures and reaffirming their commitment to love and truth.

"We are not perfect," the statement read. "We have made mistakes, but by God's grace, we are learning and growing. Our mission remains the same: to reflect the love of Christ to all people, regardless of their background or beliefs. We will continue to stand for truth, but we will do so with love, humility, and grace."

The response drew mixed reactions. Some applauded their humility, while others saw it as an admission of guilt. The media continued its attacks, but the team stood firm, refusing to retaliate or compromise their principles.

The Team Tested

The pressure began to take its toll on the team. Kayla struggled with anxiety, wondering if they had done the right thing. Pastor Clark felt anger bubbling beneath the surface, frustrated by the unfairness of the attacks. Even Jonathan began to question whether they could withstand the storm.

One evening, Sarah gathered the team for prayer. "We need to remind ourselves who we're fighting for," she said. "This isn't about us—it's about Christ. He endured far worse for us, and He promised to be with us in the fire."

As they prayed, a sense of peace settled over them. Jonathan opened his Bible to Matthew 5:11-12 and read aloud: *"Blessed are you when people insult you, persecute you and falsely say all kinds of evil against you because of Me. Rejoice and be glad, because great is your reward in heaven."*

The words renewed their resolve. They weren't fighting for their reputation or their comfort—they were fighting for the kingdom.

A Public Testimony

The legal battle culminated in a court hearing that drew national attention. Jonathan was called to testify, and as he stood before the packed courtroom, he felt the weight of the moment.

"Pastor Jonathan," the opposing lawyer began, "your church has a history of exclusion and judgment. Isn't it true that your so-called 'revival of love' is just an attempt to save face?"

Jonathan took a deep breath. "It's true that we've made mistakes. We've failed to love as Christ calls us to. But this revival isn't about saving face—it's about repentance. It's about living out the love we preach, no matter the cost."

The lawyer smirked. "And what about truth? Have you sacrificed your beliefs in the name of this 'love'?"

"Absolutely not," Jonathan replied. "Love and truth are not opposites—they're inseparable. True love doesn't compromise truth, and true truth is always spoken in love. That's what we're striving for, even when we fall short."

His words echoed in the courtroom, leaving a hush in their wake.

The Outcome

Though the lawsuit was dismissed, the attacks continued. But something surprising happened: more people began to join the movement. Pastors and congregations who had been hesitant to engage now saw the team's willingness to suffer for their mission as proof of its authenticity.

Sam, the young man with brightly dyed hair, stood up during a church service and shared his testimony. "When I first walked into this church, I felt rejected. But now, I see what real love looks like. And I want to be part of it."

His words moved the congregation to tears. One by one, other members stood to share how the revival had changed their lives.

The Team's Reflection

That evening, the team gathered at Jonathan's home. Kayla spoke first. "I was so afraid of what the world would think of us. But now I see that their attacks don't matter. What matters is staying faithful."

Pastor Clark added, "I've spent my life preaching about standing for truth, but I never realized how much it costs. And yet, I've never felt more sure that we're doing the right thing."

Jonathan looked around the room, his voice steady. "The enemy thought he could silence us with fear and division. But love is stronger than fear. And as long as we stand firm in Christ, nothing can stop what He's doing."

The team bowed their heads in prayer, united in purpose and strengthened by the trials they had faced. The ultimate test had shown them that love wasn't just their mission—it was their weapon, their shield, and their victory.

Chapter 25: Love in Action

The attacks on the team and their mission had only solidified their resolve. They knew it was time to take the revival of love beyond church walls and into the world. The team began planning an ambitious event that would unite believers across denominations in a single, powerful demonstration of Christ's love: a **Global Day of Service**.

Jonathan announced the initiative during a meeting with pastors from various denominations. "This isn't about promoting a church or a denomination. It's about showing the world what happens when we come together to serve in the name of Jesus. One day, one mission: to love our neighbors as Christ loves us."

Planning the Day

The team worked tirelessly, coordinating with churches, non-profits, and community organizations across the globe. Each participating church was encouraged to adopt a project that met the unique needs of their community—whether feeding the hungry, visiting the elderly, cleaning neighborhoods, or providing free medical services.

Kayla led the charge on communications, creating a campaign that emphasized unity and love. The slogan, **"One Day, One Mission: Love in Action,"** quickly gained traction, inspiring thousands to sign up. Social media buzzed with hashtags like #LoveInAction and #GlobalDayOfService.

Pastor Clark spearheaded training sessions, teaching volunteers how to serve with humility and grace. "This isn't about us," he reminded them. "It's about showing people Jesus through our actions."

The Day Begins

On the morning of the Global Day of Service, the team gathered in prayer. "Lord," Jonathan prayed, "let this day be a reflection of Your love. Use our hands and feet to bring healing, hope, and joy to those who need it most."

As the sun rose, volunteers across continents donned shirts bearing the event's logo and set out to serve. In cities and towns, villages and neighborhoods, the church became the hands and feet of Christ.

Stories of Service

1. **In New York City**, volunteers transformed an abandoned lot into a community garden, providing fresh produce for low-income families. A young boy who had never eaten fresh vegetables before exclaimed, "This is amazing! I didn't know food could grow like this."
2. **In Nairobi, Kenya**, a group of churches united to repair homes in a struggling village. One elderly woman, whose roof had been leaking for years, wept as the volunteers finished their work. "You've given me more than a roof—you've given me dignity," she said.
3. **In São Paulo, Brazil**, teams provided free medical clinics in underserved areas. A single mother, after receiving care for her children, said, "You've saved my family. I will never forget this."

4. **In Mumbai, India**, volunteers distributed meals to street children, sharing not just food but songs and stories of hope. "For the first time," one child said, "I feel like someone sees me."

Unity in Action

One of the most moving aspects of the day was the unity it displayed. In a world often divided by culture, language, and even religion, believers worked side by side, driven by a shared mission.

In a remote village in Eastern Europe, Catholic and Protestant volunteers, who had previously avoided each other, partnered to rebuild a school. One of the local pastors said, "Today, I realized that what divides us is nothing compared to what unites us."

In the United States, a megachurch and a small storefront congregation partnered to serve meals at a homeless shelter. One volunteer remarked, "It doesn't matter how big or small our churches are—we're one body."

The Media Takes Notice

Unlike the previous attacks, the media coverage of the Global Day of Service was overwhelmingly positive. Journalists around the world reported on the event, highlighting the acts of kindness and the unity displayed by the church.

One headline read: **"Love in Action: How the Church is Changing the World."** A television anchor commented, "In a time of division and uncertainty, this movement reminds us of the power of love to bring people together."

Even some of the team's critics were silenced, moved by the sheer scale and impact of the event.

A Celebration of Love

As the sun set on the Global Day of Service, the team gathered for a live-streamed closing event. Churches from around the world joined virtually, sharing testimonies and stories of transformation. The stream featured videos of volunteers at work, heartfelt interviews with those who had been served, and messages of encouragement from church leaders.

Jonathan addressed the global audience, his voice filled with emotion. "Today, we've seen what happens when the church becomes the hands and feet of Christ. This isn't the end—it's the beginning. Let's continue to live out love every day, showing the world who Jesus is."

The event closed with a powerful time of worship, as believers from every corner of the globe lifted their voices together in praise.

The Team's Reflection

That evening, the team gathered around a bonfire, reflecting on the day's events. Kayla spoke first. "Today, I saw what the church is capable of when we stop fighting and start loving. It's beautiful."

Pastor Clark, his usual sternness softened, nodded. "I've spent years preaching about standing for truth, but today reminded me that truth without love isn't truth at all. This is the gospel in action."

Sarah added, "We've been through so much—attacks, criticism, doubts—but today, it was worth it. I think the world caught a glimpse of Christ."

Jonathan looked around the circle, his heart full. "This is what we've been working for. But it's not just one day. If we want this revival to last, we need to keep living it out."

A Movement That Lasts

The Global Day of Service marked a turning point in the revival. It showed the world—and the church—that love wasn't just a concept or a sermon topic. It was an action, a way of life, and a reflection of Christ.

As the fire crackled and the stars shone above, the team knew their work wasn't finished. The flame of love had been reignited, but now it was up to the church to keep it burning.

And they were ready to keep fighting—not with weapons of the world, but with the unstoppable power of love in action.

Chapter 26: The Final Push

The Global Day of Service had sent shockwaves through churches and communities worldwide. Yet, as the flame of love spread, so did resistance. The team could feel the pressure mounting—something darker was stirring. The attacks from the media, legal challenges, and spiritual fatigue weren't random. They were part of a calculated effort by the enemy to extinguish the revival before it fully took hold.

Jonathan called the team together one evening, his face grave. "This isn't just about opposition from people or systems. This is spiritual warfare, and it's time we confront the root of the resistance directly."

The Team Prepares

The team spent the next week preparing for an intense period of prayer, fasting, and intercession. They sought guidance from Scripture, drawing strength from passages about spiritual warfare:

- **Ephesians 6:12:** *"For we wrestle not against flesh and blood, but against principalities, against powers, against the rulers of the darkness of this world, against spiritual wickedness in high places."*
- **2 Corinthians 10:4-5:** *"The weapons we fight with are not the weapons of the world. On the contrary, they have divine power to demolish strongholds."*

Each member took time to examine their own hearts, repenting of anything that might hinder their unity or effectiveness. Pastor Clark, who had once struggled with pride, confessed his need to fully surrender to God's will. Kayla, who had battled fear, declared her trust in God's power over the enemy.

Father Martinez led them in prayer, his voice steady. "Lord, we come before You in humility, knowing that this battle is not ours but Yours. Equip us with Your armor, fill us with Your Spirit, and guide us as we stand against the forces of darkness."

A Night of Intercession

The team gathered at Grace Community Church one Friday night, joined by intercessors from various congregations. The sanctuary was dimly lit, the atmosphere heavy with expectation. They knelt, stood, and paced as they prayed, each voice lifting a plea to heaven.

As the hours passed, the spiritual intensity increased. Kayla began to see flashes of the demonic realm again. Shadowy figures moved in the periphery of her vision, whispering lies and accusations.

"They're trying to distract us," she said aloud. "They know they're losing ground."

Jonathan read aloud from **Psalm 91**, declaring God's protection and victory. "*For He will command His angels concerning you to guard you in all your ways.*"

A Breakthrough Vision

Suddenly, Kayla gasped and fell to her knees. Her voice trembled as she described what she saw:
"There's a massive fortress—dark, oppressive, covered in

chains. Inside, I see people trapped, crying out for help. But outside... there's light breaking through. It's coming from us—from the prayers of God's people. The walls are cracking."

Pastor Clark's voice rose, filled with determination. "We're not stopping now. The enemy's stronghold is breaking, but we need to keep pressing."

The team formed a circle, their hands joined as they prayed with renewed fervor. They called out strongholds by name: division, fear, pride, apathy, and complacency. They declared the power of Christ's love to demolish every barrier.

A Heavenly Response

As their prayers reached a crescendo, the room seemed to shift. Kayla saw the chains in her vision begin to snap, one by one. The fortress crumbled as a brilliant light filled the space, driving out the darkness.

She whispered, "The captives are free. The enemy is retreating."

At that moment, an overwhelming sense of peace and victory filled the sanctuary. The team fell silent, their hearts awed by the power of God's presence. They had confronted the enemy, not with weapons of the world, but with the spiritual weapons of prayer, faith, and love—and they had seen victory.

The Aftermath

The following day, reports began pouring in from churches worldwide. Congregations that had been struggling with division found themselves united. Pastors who had been on the verge of burnout were renewed in their passion. Families that had been fractured experienced unexpected reconciliation.

One pastor wrote to the team: "I don't know what happened last night, but during our prayer service, we felt something break in the spiritual realm. It was like a cloud lifted, and we could finally see clearly again."

Jonathan read the message aloud, his voice choked with emotion. "This is the power of prayer. This is what happens when we fight the real battle."

The Team's Reflection

That evening, the team gathered to reflect on what they had experienced. Pastor Clark, who had been skeptical of spiritual warfare in the past, spoke first. "I've always believed in prayer, but tonight, I saw its power in a way I never imagined. This was real. The enemy was real. And so is our victory."

Kayla nodded. "For so long, I was afraid of the darkness. But now I see—it's no match for the light of Christ. We don't fight alone."

Jonathan looked around the room, his face filled with gratitude. "This isn't the end. The enemy will try again, but now we know how to fight. Love is our weapon, and prayer is our battlefield."

A Final Push

The team knew the battle wasn't over, but they were ready for whatever came next. They had seen the strongholds of the enemy crumble, not by their own strength but by the power of God working through them.

The revival of love was no longer a fragile flame—it was a blazing fire, spreading across the world. And with each prayer, each act of love, and each step of faith, they were preparing the church for its ultimate purpose: to be the Bride of Christ, ready and waiting for her Groom.

Chapter 27: The Bride Awakens

The weeks following the spiritual battle were unlike anything the team had ever experienced. Across the world, churches began to reflect the transformation that had started as a small flicker of revival. The Body of Christ, once fractured by division, pride, and complacency, was awakening to its true calling. The Bride of Christ was beginning to shine.

A Unified Body

In cities, towns, and villages, churches from different denominations joined together in unprecedented ways. Instead of competing for members or debating doctrine, they worked side by side, driven by a shared mission: to love God and love others.

In one city, a Catholic parish hosted a joint prayer service with a nearby Pentecostal church. The sight of priests and worship leaders standing shoulder to shoulder moved many to tears.

In a rural community, Methodist and Baptist congregations partnered to rebuild homes destroyed by a recent storm. One homeowner, overwhelmed by their generosity, remarked, "I don't care what church you're from—you're showing me Jesus."

Jonathan and the team traveled to see these collaborations firsthand. Each story reaffirmed what they had prayed for: the church was becoming one, just as Christ had prayed in John 17.

Love in Action

The revival of love wasn't limited to church partnerships—it spilled into the streets, schools, workplaces, and homes. Members of the church began living out their faith in tangible ways:

- **In a struggling neighborhood**, believers started a free childcare program, allowing single parents to work without worry.
- **In a corporate setting**, employees began organizing lunchtime prayer meetings, transforming the atmosphere of their workplace.
- **In a broken family**, a father who had been estranged from his children for years sought forgiveness, inspired by the love he saw in his church community.

Kayla, who had been deeply impacted by the vision of the Bride stained by pride, saw glimpses of the transformation she had longed for. "This is it," she said one evening, tears streaming down her face. "This is what the church is supposed to look like."

A Global Gathering

To celebrate what God was doing, the team organized a global event they called **The Bride Awakens.** Churches from every denomination and nation were invited to participate in a live-streamed worship service, celebrating the unity and love that had taken hold.

The event was held in a massive stadium, with thousands in attendance and millions watching online. Worship teams from different traditions led the crowd in praise, blending hymns, contemporary songs, and even traditional chants into a seamless expression of unity.

Jonathan stepped onto the stage, his heart pounding as he addressed the crowd. "Tonight, we celebrate what God has done," he began. "The church is awakening—not to programs, not to traditions, but to her identity as the Bride of Christ. We are His, and He is ours."

He read from Revelation 19:7-8:
"Let us rejoice and be glad and give Him glory! For the wedding of the Lamb has come, and His Bride has made herself ready. Fine linen, bright and clean, was given her to wear."

As he finished, the crowd erupted into applause, not for him, but for the One who had made it all possible.

Testimonies of Transformation

During the event, testimonies poured in from around the world. A young woman in Asia shared how her church had reconciled with a neighboring congregation after decades of animosity. A man from the Middle East described how believers from different cultural backgrounds had come together to provide aid to refugees.

One pastor from South America summed it up: "We've stopped focusing on what divides us and started focusing on what unites us—Jesus. And now, the world is starting to see Him in us."

The Vision Fulfilled

Kayla, who had once been hesitant about her role in the revival, felt the weight of her earlier vision coming full circle. During the worship, she closed her eyes and saw the Bride again—this time, radiant and whole. Her gown, once torn and stained, was now spotless, glowing with a light that seemed to come from within.

"She's ready," Kayla whispered. "The Bride is waking up."

A Commission to Continue

As the event came to a close, Jonathan and the team stood together on stage. Pastor Clark, once rigid and skeptical, spoke with newfound humility. "This isn't the end of the journey—it's the beginning. The church has awakened, but we must stay vigilant. Love isn't a moment—it's a way of life."

Father Martinez added, "We've seen what's possible when we're united. Let's continue to walk in humility, love, and faith, showing the world what it means to be the Body of Christ."

Jonathan closed the event with a prayer of dedication. "Lord, thank You for awakening Your Bride. Keep us united, keep us humble, and keep us focused on You. Let the love You've poured into us overflow to a world in desperate need. We are Yours, now and forever. Amen."

A World Changed

The revival of love didn't end that night. It continued to spread, transforming not just churches but entire communities. The

Bride of Christ was no longer fragmented or distracted—she was unified, radiant, and ready for her Groom.

As the team parted ways, each returning to their own communities, they carried with them the lessons they had learned. They knew the work wasn't finished, but they were confident in the One who had started it.

The Bride had awakened, and the world would never be the same.

Chapter 28: The World is Watching

The revival of love that had started as a flicker was now a blazing fire, illuminating churches, communities, and nations. The transformation of the Body of Christ was no longer a hidden work—it was undeniable. People from all walks of life, many of whom had once been skeptical or hostile to Christianity, began to take notice. The world was watching, and what they saw was changing hearts.

An Unstoppable Movement

The Global Day of Service, the unity among churches, and the stories of radical love had created ripples that reached far beyond the church. News outlets that had once criticized the team's efforts were now running stories about the tangible impact of the revival.

One prominent journalist, who had written a scathing article dismissing the movement as "idealistic nonsense," published a retraction. "I've spent years pointing out the flaws of the church," he wrote. "But what I'm seeing now is something I can't explain—lives changed, communities healed, and a love that seems otherworldly. Perhaps I've been wrong."

Social media was flooded with stories of forgiveness, reconciliation, and selfless acts of love. The hashtag #LoveInAction became a global trend, with millions sharing their experiences of how the church's revival had touched their lives.

Conversions Begin

At first, the conversions trickled in—individuals moved by the love they had seen in the church. But soon, the trickle became a flood. In cities and towns around the world, people began flocking to churches, not because of flashy events or persuasive arguments, but because they had seen the love of God in action.

- In **Los Angeles**, a group of former gang members gave their lives to Christ after witnessing a local church's relentless outreach efforts in their neighborhood.
- In **Tokyo**, a high-ranking business executive publicly declared his faith, saying, "I've seen success, but it was empty. What I see in the church is real—it's love, and it's something only God can give."
- In **Cairo**, a Muslim family, moved by the kindness of Christian neighbors during a crisis, began attending a local house church. They later shared their testimony of encountering Jesus in a dream.

Kayla, reading these reports, was overwhelmed with emotion. "This is what we've prayed for. The world isn't just hearing about God's love—they're seeing it."

Mass Gatherings of Faith

As the movement gained momentum, mass gatherings began to spring up organically. In parks, stadiums, and city squares, people gathered to worship, pray, and share testimonies of how God's love had changed their lives.

In one remarkable event in **Rio de Janeiro**, more than 100,000 people filled a beach to celebrate the revival. As the crowd sang, "How Great is Our God," the atmosphere was electric. Thousands came forward to give their lives to Christ, many weeping as they experienced His love for the first time.

At a similar event in **Johannesburg**, a young woman who had been contemplating suicide shared her story. "I was at the end of my rope," she said, her voice trembling. "But then I saw what the church was doing in my community. I thought, 'If God's love can change them, maybe it can change me too.' And it has."

The Power of Love

The conversions weren't limited to those who had never known Christ. Many who had walked away from the church because of its failures were returning, drawn by the authenticity of the revival. One man, a former pastor who had left the ministry in disillusionment, said, "I've been bitter for years, but seeing the church truly live out love has reminded me of why I followed Jesus in the first place."

Even prominent skeptics began to question their assumptions. During a televised debate, an atheist professor admitted, "I don't believe in God, but I can't deny that something extraordinary is happening. The love these people show—it's not natural. It's... compelling."

Jonathan, watching the debate with the team, whispered, "That's the power of God's love. It's irresistible."

A Global Testimony

The team decided to organize a global testimony event, inviting people from every continent to share how the revival had impacted their lives. Broadcast live, the event featured stories from every corner of the globe:

- A woman in **India** who had been healed emotionally after forgiving her abusive father.
- A soldier in **Ukraine** who had found peace and hope in the middle of conflict after encountering a group of praying believers.
- A man in **Australia** who had been on the verge of bankruptcy, only to be rescued by the generosity of a local church.

As the event drew to a close, Jonathan addressed the global audience. "This isn't about us," he said. "This is about Jesus. He is the source of this love. He is the One changing lives. And He invites everyone—no matter who you are, no matter what you've done—to experience His love."

The Team's Reflection

That night, the team gathered to reflect on what they had witnessed. Pastor Clark, who had once doubted the mission's effectiveness, spoke first. "I've preached my whole life about God's power to transform lives. But seeing it on this scale... it's beyond anything I imagined."

Reverend Harris nodded. "This is what the church was meant to be. Not a building, not a program, but a movement of love that points people to Christ."

Kayla, her voice filled with emotion, said, "When we started this journey, I never thought it would lead here. But now I see—God's love isn't just for the church. It's for the world."

Jonathan stood, his heart full. "The world is watching, and they're seeing Jesus in us. That's what this is all about."

A World Changed Forever

The revival of love had awakened the church, unified believers, and transformed communities. But its greatest impact was the millions of lives that had been forever changed by the power of God's love.

As the team bowed their heads in prayer, Jonathan whispered, "Lord, thank You for letting us be part of this. Keep us faithful. Keep us humble. And let the world continue to see You through us."

The world was watching, and the light of Christ was shining brighter than ever. The Bride of Christ, radiant and full of love, was preparing for her Groom—and the world was being drawn to Him like never before.

Epilogue: Love Restored

The church stood at the crossroads of eternity, fully awakened and alive with purpose. The revival of love that had begun as a desperate cry for change had grown into a global movement, reshaping the Body of Christ into what it was always meant to be—a radiant Bride, prepared for her Groom. The church had rediscovered its first love, not through programs or strategies, but through repentance, unity, and a relentless pursuit of Christ.

The Church in Balance

Across the world, believers lived out the gospel with renewed passion. No longer divided by denominations or distracted by petty disputes, the church worked as one body, unified in love and truth. Where once there had been discord, now there was harmony; where pride had flourished, now humility reigned.

Communities once plagued by despair and division were now places of hope and restoration. Entire neighborhoods were transformed as the church became the hands and feet of Christ, meeting physical, emotional, and spiritual needs. The balance the world had so desperately needed had been restored, as the light of the church pushed back the darkness.

The Final Mission

The team, now scattered across the globe, continued their work, each serving as a steward of the revival. Jonathan remained at Grace Community Church, now a model of unity and discipleship. Kayla traveled to regions where the gospel was still resisted, bringing the message of love and hope to those in spiritual darkness. Pastor Clark focused on training the next generation of leaders, while Father Martinez worked tirelessly to bridge gaps between denominations.

In their hearts, they knew the ultimate goal had been fulfilled. The church was no longer a fragmented institution—it was the Bride of Christ, prepared for the moment when the heavens would open and the Groom would call her home.

The World is Watching

Even as the world descended further into chaos, the church stood as a beacon of light. Wars, disasters, and moral decay continued to plague the nations, but the church's love and faithfulness provided balance and hope. Non-believers turned to the church in unprecedented numbers, drawn not by eloquent arguments but by the undeniable evidence of transformed lives.

"Your love is what convinced me," one man said during a testimony at Grace Community. "I didn't need a sermon. I needed to see something real—and I found it in you."

Love Restored

As Jonathan stood in the sanctuary one evening, reflecting on the journey that had brought the church to this moment, he opened his Bible to Revelation 2:4-5, the passage that had first convicted him so deeply.
"Yet I hold this against you: You have forsaken the love you had at first. Consider how far you have fallen! Repent and do the things you did at first."

He smiled, tears in his eyes. "We've done it, Lord. We've returned to our first love. And now we're ready—ready for You."

The Bride is Ready

Kayla, on the other side of the world, knelt in prayer in a small house church. In her mind, the vision of the Bride returned—this time, she was more radiant than ever, clothed in a gown of pure white. Her face was lifted, her eyes fixed on the horizon, waiting for her Groom.

"The time is near," Kayla whispered, a sense of peace washing over her. "The Bride is ready."

A Glimpse of Eternity

The church, fully awakened and restored, had fulfilled its mission. It had balanced the world, becoming the salt and light it was always meant to be. It had embraced love, not as a fleeting emotion but as a lifestyle rooted in Christ. And now, it waited with eager anticipation for the rapture, for the moment when the Bride and Groom would be united forever.

A Final Prayer

As the sun set over the world, a prayer rose from countless voices across nations, cultures, and languages—a single, unified cry of love and devotion.

"Come, Lord Jesus."

The church had rediscovered her first love, fulfilled her mission, and prepared herself for eternity. The Bride was ready. The world had seen the power of God's love. And the Groom was coming soon.

Made in the USA
Columbia, SC
26 November 2024

47205036R00079